AGE
OF
UN-
REASON

The X Gang Series

Recipe for Hate
New Dark Ages
Age of Unreason

WARREN KINSELLA

THE X GANG

DUNDURN
TORONTO

Publisher: Scott Fraser | Editor: Allison Hirst
Cover designer: Laura Boyle
Cover image: Shutterstock.com/Robert Spriggs
Printer: Webcom, a division of Marquis Book Printing Inc.

Library and Archives Canada Cataloguing in Publication

Title: Age of un-reason / Warren Kinsella.
Other titles: Age of unreason
Names: Kinsella, Warren, 1960- author.
Series: Kinsella, Warren, 1960- X Gang.
Description: Series statement: The X-Gang
Identifiers: Canadiana (print) 20190196513 | Canadiana (ebook) 20190196521 | ISBN 9781459742185 (softcover) | ISBN 9781459742192 (PDF) | ISBN 9781459742208 (EPUB)
Classification: LCC PS8621.I59 A64 2019 | DDC jC813/.6—dc23

We acknowledge the support of the Canada Council for the Arts and the Ontario Arts Council for our publishing program. We also acknowledge the financial support of the Government of Ontario, through the Ontario Book Publishing Tax Credit and Ontario Creates, and the Government of Canada.

Printed and bound in Canada.

VISIT US AT

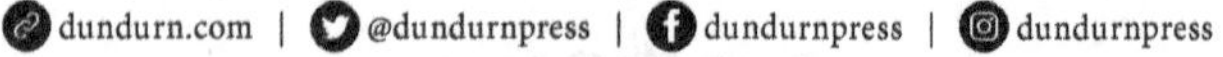

Dundurn
3 Church Street, Suite 500
Toronto, Ontario, Canada
M5E 1M2

For Emma, Ben, Sam, Jacob

APRIL 13

Words. That's all these are, David. Words. Darkening, dry leaves — turned brown and black, blowing around on her school's painted, grey-white concrete playground. A wedge of geese, way, way up, pinned against a glittering blanket of Maine sky. Scratches on a piece of paper, like the pricks of buckthorn on my pale extended arm as ten-year-old me runs to the edge of the forest, escaping.

Just words. That's all they are, David: words. Filaments, figments, fictions.

But words have defined the boundaries of my life, every luckless minute of it. Words now propel me forward, toward what I must do next. Without stopping, without pity.

Words are what you make of them. Me? Words made and make ME.

Today, my words — and this, my manifesto — will be written all over the streets.

In blood. And in tears.

CHAPTER 1

The words contained in the police report were leaked everywhere. They were on the front page of every newspaper.

The yellow Ford truck had quietly pulled up to the curb around 8:20 a.m. on Monday, April 13, 1981. It slid into a spot just a little bit past the entrance to 70 Forest Avenue in Portland, Maine. Back in the 1920s, someone had carved the words "YOUNG MEN'S CHRISTIAN ASSOCIATION" into the grey foundation stones. But the old building was now home to the YWCA — the men had moved to a much more modern space down the road.

The old building was a bit of a dump, and it creaked and wheezed like an old man. Its best feature was the main doors, positioned as they were beneath a spectacular archway, which architects called a *lunette*. This area was decorated with lovely leaded glass, which shimmered when the sun caught it.

Most weekdays it was pretty challenging to find a parking spot so close to the main doors. But not that day. The driver of the yellow truck had no difficulty finding a space. He'd been watching the place for weeks, the police figured, and he knew how busy it could be early in the morning.

The staff greeted one another as they arrived for work. It was an unusually warm spring day, and some of them were smiling and chattering about their weekends. Some paused to hold the door open for harried-looking parents dropping off their kids at the Y's daycare.

The truck, it was later discovered, was the legal property of Roger Rentals of Boston, Massachusetts, but it had been assigned to a rental company — Macmillan's Body Shop — way up in Newport, Vermont, near the Canadian border. A pair of bewildered employees at Macmillan's would tell a small army of FBI agents that the truck had been driven off the lot a few days before the bombing, rented by a clean-cut young man who identified himself as Thomas M. Jones from Pulaski, Tennessee. Mr. Jones had told them he was helping a friend move. *Thomas M. Jones* was, in fact, the name of a long-dead lawyer, in whose offices the Ku Klux Klan was formed in Pulaski back in 1865. Jones had started the Klan along with some fellow former Confederate soldiers, mainly as a lark.

This modern-day Thomas M. Jones was a slender young man with a crew cut. When he smiled — which he apparently didn't do a lot when he was at

Macmillan's — he had a broad, toothy grin that made him look like a teenager.

The five-story YWCA building had an ancient gym located on the main floor along with the daycare center. The administration and membership offices were housed on the second. On the upper floors were offices supporting an array of programs from summer camps to healthy living to veterans outreach. There were also a couple of converted classrooms, where the YWCA and YMCA did a booming business offering ESL classes for a modest fee. The women's health and well-being offices were up there, too. They offered women and girls advice on reproductive health.

The investigators discovered that for the four days prior to the bombing, Thomas M. Jones had been renting a room at the Holiday Inn across the road from the Maine Mall in South Portland. He'd parked the yellow rental truck in the lot out back, in a spot that could be readily seen from his room. On the inn's register, he had used the long-dead Klansman's name, but it turned out he had entered a real mailing address in the registry: a P.O. box in Mobile, Alabama. The FBI would quickly determine, however, that the P.O. box was registered to the United Klans of America. The man had paid cash for his room and didn't leave behind a single fingerprint or anything else that gave any hint to his true identity.

That Monday morning, the man everyone would soon know as Thomas M. Jones drove the yellow rental truck downtown and parked it on Forest Avenue.

He then hopped out of the truck, locked the door, and walked west.

Soon after he regained consciousness at Mercy Hospital, security guard Bob Cox was interviewed by the police and FBI. He immediately began recounting all of his injuries to the FBI agents. "The doc says I've got more than three hundred stitches outside my body, fellas, and more than six hundred inside. He told me they also had to leave three or four clamps inside me, to hold together the muscle and tissue and whatnot. They operated on me for a full day, on what was my first wedding anniversary. How about that, eh?" He paused and looked at the agents.

They said nothing. They were there to talk to the security guard about whether he had seen anything. Bob Cox wasn't going anywhere anytime soon, but they needed to get his statement as soon as possible.

Cox sensed this and stopped rambling. "How many, fellas?"

The agents looked at each other. "As of this morning, a hundred and twenty dead," one of them finally said. "Three hundred injured."

Bob Cox, who had worked on the main floor at the YWCA and knew the names of each of the children in the daycare and many of their parents, started to cry.

His big frame shook the hospital bed. Although it hurt when he moved, he couldn't stop crying.

As it turned out, Mr. Cox was the only survivor to see the young man who called himself Thomas M. Jones step out of the yellow rental truck that morning and walk away.

Cox was thirty-three years old, newly married, and was a volunteer peewee hockey league referee in South Portland. He had just arrived for his regular shift at the Y when he spotted the truck. "It was weird," Cox would tell the FBI, "for someone to park a truck that big in that spot at that time of day."

He'd watched the man for a second or two — even thought about telling him to park somewhere else, so parents would have an easier time dropping off their kids — but then he remembered he'd left his lunch back in his van, parked in the municipal lot a block away. He forgot about the truck and the man and instead doubled back to retrieve it. On his way back, he said he stopped to talk to the parking lot attendant about the Red Sox before heading back in the direction of the Y. He was half a block away when the bomb went off.

He said he couldn't actually remember what sound it made; if anything, there seemed to be an *absence* of sound, he recalled, a momentary silence that preceded the opening of the Gates of Hell. He remembered an enormous ball of fire, far bigger than the truck had been, pushing outward. Then he was hit with the blast wave, which Bob Cox said he could almost see, like a living thing, as it tore through everything.

Some of the nice old trees out front of the YWCA bent then broke into a million pieces, embedding themselves in asphalt, surrounding buildings, parked vehicles, and bystanders. Windows along Forest Avenue exploded and the shards of glass became searing-hot missiles. They sounded like music, Bob Cox recalled thinking. Like chimes, he said.

One moment, the Y's staff, parents and kids, and other residents were heading to work or school or wherever; the next, they were just *gone*. All that remained was a beast shaped like fire, twisting and screeching and casting out billowing black smoke and choking dust.

Cox recalled hearing the sound of a car horn echoing in the distance as debris rained down on the scorched pavement. Next he heard the wailing of a child crying out for her mother. It was only after what seemed like a very long time that the screams of the wounded commenced.

The Ford truck was no longer there, of course. It had delivered its cargo of death and then it was gone. A massive crater remained where Jones had parked it. Parts of the truck were later found as much as five blocks away. A janitor found one of the truck's axles on the roof of a school two streets over.

The old building that housed the YWCA had been leveled. Thick steel cables could be seen in the concrete slabs that had once supported the structure. Bricks and bits of mortar littered Forest Avenue as far as Bob Cox could see.

He'd been in shock, he figured, because he didn't recall immediately feeling any pain at all. The blast had flung him up against the passenger door of a station wagon, as if he were a paper doll. After looking up and down the street for someone to help, Cox had looked down at his own injuries and promptly fainted.

CHAPTER 2

X was a man of few words.

I had been at the shithole motel on Sanibel Island, getting my arm ready for blast-off, when X called. I knew right away it was something bad, because we hadn't talked in a while — a long while.

"Hey, X," I said, genuinely happy to hear from him. He was still my best friend, after all. "To what do I owe this pleasure?"

His voice was flat, all business. He didn't sound particularly happy to be speaking to me. He was calling from Portland, he said.

"I figured," I said.

"Have you seen the news?"

"Not really," I said, electing not to mention I'd been busy procuring some junk from my guy in the 7-Eleven parking lot across the causeway. I looked around the dark motel room where I'd been hiding out for two weeks. "I don't have a TV. Why? What's up?"

The line hissed like a snake. "Kurt ..." he said finally — alarm bells immediately went off, because he never used my first name, or *anyone's* first name; he somehow regarded it as too intimate or something. I held my breath. "Eddie and Nagamo are dead."

Eddie was Eddie Igglesden, the drummer in my band, the Hot Nasties. And Nagamo was his girlfriend, a Canadian who was in another punk band. The two of them had been together since our tour the year before.

"What? When?" I'm not sure why I thought it was important to ask him when it had happened. I wasn't thinking straight, I guess. Momentarily, I even forgot about the bindle of smack beside me on the shitty little bed in the shitty little motel room.

"This morning," X said. "They were at the old Y on Forest. A bomb went off."

I felt sick, like I was actually going to puke. "What bomb, man? What the fuck are you talking about?" The room spun and buckled like I was in an earthquake.

"Someone set off a bomb at the YWCA on Forest this morning, Kurt," he said, using my name again. "Eddie and Nagamo were there for an appointment."

"What kind of appointment?" I asked. "What —"

X cut me off. "Nagamo thought she was pregnant. So, they'd gone there to get advice about that." Pause.

"Shit," I said, and started to cry. "I can't believe this." I dropped the phone onto the filthy carpet. I was gasping. I could still hear X's voice coming through the line.

"Kurt?" he was saying, "Kurt, you need to come home. *Kurt, are you there?*"

I wasn't — "there," that is. I was elsewhere. Gone. I had been for a while. I didn't pick the phone back up, the conversation over.

The past couple years had been *fucking nuts*. First our friend Jimmy Cleary got killed by a neo-Nazi psychopath. Then our friend Danny O'Heran killed a neo-Nazi psychopath and got killed himself. And then our record label dropped us. And there was all kinds of other shit along the way: death threats, beatings, bad press, interpersonal psychodrama. It was relentless, and it got to me. It broke me. It chewed me up and spit me out like gum that's lost its taste. And, yes, sure, I was a punk. I was supposed to be tough, right? But I was broken.

I'd been in the band Social Blemishes when it all started, and then I joined the Hot Nasties after Jimmy died. And for a while I was on top of the punk rock world — signed to Stiff Records, playing sold-out shows all over the place. We were going to record a single or two for Stiff, tour some more, then maybe make an album. We had the tunes, too, great tunes. We knew how to play, you know?

And then Stiff stiffed us. After seeking us out — after telling *us* they believed in *us* — they dropped us. It was Jake Riviera, the big cheese, calling all the way from London, England. He spoke to Sam Shiller, our lead guitarist, and he cut to the chase. "Sam, I'm sorry. The punk-pop thing just isn't happening right now.

Everything is this new wave shite. That's what the college kids want. We're exercising our option."

And that was that. They let us keep the advance they'd given us, at least, which was a good thing, to tell you the truth, because we'd already spent it — on new amps, guitars, and Schott Perfecto biker jackets like the ones the Ramones wear. Not cheap.

And yeah, it's true, some of it went up my nose, too. And what little was left of my share made its way into my arm (or behind my knee, or in the bottom of my feet).

Heroin had become my best girlfriend. And I'm not even into girls.

But I'm getting ahead of myself. I've lost the narrative. I've lost the storyline. I'm sick, I'm lost, I'm lonely. I'm living in Motel Shithole on Sanibel Island, Florida, and I wash dishes at the family-friendly Lazy Dolphin on Periwinkle Way. And I'm a junkie. Allegedly.

You see, I have totally screwed things up, deeply disappointing my family and bandmates and friends. Especially my best friend, X. I could see the disappointment in his eyes before I left.

X, with pupils darker than his darkest Converse Chucks, blacker than the tops of his shiniest Doc Martens boots; one bigger than the other, frozen that way after he was jumped by two guys at a community hall gig. I couldn't get to him in time; I was dealing with a couple of foot-swinging skinhead *bovver* boys myself.

He would lock that uneven gaze on me, and I'd just stop. More than once, mid-song, I'd look over to the side of the stage, or down in the pit, where punks would be slam-dancing in a frenzy of sweat and spit, with X hovering at the periphery, to make sure no one got hurt, and I'd catch his eyes on me, and I'd just *stop playing*, with the rest of the Hot Nasties glaring at me, wondering *what now, Kurt?*

It seemed X was always mad at me for something. Like the speed thing, which put me in the hospital in Toronto, or the heroin thing, which put me beside a sink in a seafood restaurant on the Gulf of Mexico in deepest Florida — sniffing, coughing, wasting away, calculating the dishes-washed to smack-purchased ratio (with minimum wage winning me about thirty bucks a day, I'd usually have ten bucks left over for food).

X was my best friend. He didn't care that I was gay; he didn't care that I was a fuck-up. But he could just glance at me with that laser-beam look, and I'd catch my breath and the universe would immediately be in a state of upheaval. Since grade seven at Holy Cross, when he introduced himself to me in the school gym at lunchtime. It had been like the moon revealing the sun after an eclipse: it was a big fucking deal for me when we became best friends.

I loved him and he pissed me off, all at the same time, you know?

X was Mr. Straight Edge — no drugs, no tobacco, no booze, no nothing. Me? There wasn't much I wouldn't snort, swallow, or shoot up.

Don't get me wrong: it wasn't that X judged me, but he also kind of did. It wasn't that my best friend would act like he was superior or anything like that. But deep down, I think I actually *wanted* him to judge me, to yell at me. I wanted him to realign the aforementioned universe for me. I wanted him to fix everything. Because I didn't know how. Not anymore.

The room whirled around me, a merry-go-round off its axis, the phone on the dirty carpet making that jarring hang-me-up sound.

I squinted at the little baggie of junk beside it, pondering.

"Let's fuck one last time."

CHAPTER 3

X called me back the next day to make sure I was okay. I told him I'd see what I could do about getting home. I'd have to pry some dough out of my dad. He wouldn't be happy.

When X told me he was with Patti and Betty in the Kowalchuks' basement, I could picture it, every single detail. Over against one wall the puny amps the girls had picked up in a garage sale and a near-useless drum kit they'd found on someone's curb on garbage day. The amps and drum kits were covered in skull-and-crossbones stickers. There were some old Fender copies, too, but they didn't look like they'd been used in a long time. The Punk Rock Virgins had graduated to better instruments — real Fenders, real Mosrites. Beside all that were some dusty boxes that their dad had brought home years earlier and forgotten about. He was a marine biologist or something. Someone had written "TTX" on the side of one of the boxes, which Sister Betty had actually turned into a song, "True to X"; she called it a funny punk-pop number about her sister's true love for my friend X. Next to that, an old typewriter on top of some suitcases, and a stack of plain white paper and maybe a box of envelopes beside it. This, I knew, was the typewriter the Upchuck sisters used to hammer out lyrics for their songs, most of which were about feminism. I loved that the Virgins typed up their lyrics. Unlike the rest of us — in the Hot Nasties and the Social Blemishes. We'd just scrawl out some words on bits of paper. But the Virgins — mainly Sister Betty, I think — typed them up and kept them in a three-hole binder. I loved that.

After occasional fights with my mom, I'd crash on the old couch, the one where X and the Upchuck sisters were probably sitting.

Anyway, bottom line, I wasn't there, but I should have been.

X hung up and looked at the Kowalchuk sisters, aka Patti and Betty Upchuck. They were sitting on the dilapidated old couch in the basement of the Kowalchuk family home on Sandy Road in Portland.

"Is he coming back?" Sister Betty asked. "Kurt's coming back, right?"

X looked away. "He says he is. But he has to get money from his dad first."

Sister Betty wiped streaks of smudged mascara from her face. "I can send him money," she said. "I can wire it to him from the Western Union ..."

X looked at her and shook his head. Sister Betty nodded sadly. "Right. Sending Kurt money directly is a bad idea."

"I did this," Patti said suddenly, covering her face.

X looked at her, then at her sister.

Sister Betty explained to X that they'd found out that Nagamo thought she was pregnant. Being a recent transplant to Portland, Nagamo had no other friends in town, so she'd confided in them. She said she was late and didn't know where to turn.

Patti told her to go to the Y on Forest. "They're amazing, and they won't give a shit that you're a teenager or that you're from Canada," she'd told her. "All you need is what they call informed consent. You're informed, and you consent. So go."

Patti didn't mention to Nagamo how she knew about the clinic, but X knew. Long before they'd become friends, Patti had been raped late one night near the Maine Mall after she'd finished her shift at the Orange Julius and was waiting for the bus. Two guys had pulled her into their car and assaulted her. When they were finished, they pushed her back out onto the ground of the parking lot, laughing, and drove away.

Patti had been terrified she was pregnant, so she made the journey downtown twice to the Y and the family planning clinic. The women there had been wonderful and kind, and they were the ones who had finally confirmed the good news: she wasn't carrying a rapist's baby.

Sister Betty said she was a bit surprised when her sister had given Nagamo a big hug. The two had never been close. In fact, when they first met — at the Horseshoe Tavern in Toronto, when Nagamo's all-girl punk band, Tit Sweat, had been doing a sound check — Nagamo had made a move on X, telling him, as everyone, including Patti, stood at the Horseshoe's bar, that she wanted to screw him. Just like that. When X didn't say anything right away — like, for example, "no thanks" — Patti had taken off to stay with a friend who lived in Toronto. Patti at that point had probably totally hated Nagamo's guts.

"Does Eddie know?" Patti had asked her.

Nagamo nodded. "Yeah. He's actually been awesome. Said he'd back me whatever I decided. Every step of the way, whatever happens."

Patti laughed. "Eddie Igglesden — who would've expected that?"

Nagamo laughed, too. "Yeah, from a punk rock drummer from Maine," she said, "it's something I never expected either."

Patti gave Nagamo the clinic's address and phone number, and another hug. Nagamo had asked to use Patti and Betty's phone and called right away to book an appointment for the following Monday at 9:00 a.m., when the clinic opened.

Patti started weeping again. “Fuck, X,” she said. “They’re dead because I told them to go to the Y. *I fucking killed them.*”

Sister Betty got up and knelt down beside her sister and hugged her. X reached over and put an arm around Patti, too.

CHAPTER 4

Can a punk rock star be washed up at the age of twenty-one?

I sure as shit was.

I mean, there I stood at the pay phone in the parking lot at Huxter's on Periwinkle, a stack of quarters resembling the barrel of a gun balanced on top of the phone.

Even wearing my knock-off Ray-Bans, the south Florida sun stung my eyes. I looked down. I was wearing a pair of cutoff jeans and a stained yellow Sanibel Island T-shirt I got for a buck at a tourist trap down the road. Above "SANIBEL ISLAND" I had written in marker "I HATE." The jeans were too big on me because I'd lost so much weight. As I waited for my dad to come back on the line, I notched my belt tighter.

It was the second call I'd made to my father. On the first, he'd sounded more sad than mad. As expected, he had politely declined to wire me money to buy a plane ticket. He didn't say why, and I didn't ask. We both knew all or part of the money would just go in my arm or up my nose. So, he said he'd try to arrange for the ticket to be waiting for me at the Fort Myers airport. But he needed time to arrange that, he said. I said I'd call him back.

Between calls, I'd gone into the convenience store side of Huxter's. Usually, I only frequented the side where they sold booze and where I'd sometimes buy Sibirskaya Strong vodka, the cheapest shit they had. Today, however, standing on the store side, I squinted at the papers stacked beside the cash register. The clerk, a leathery old reptile snapping gum and dead-ending a butt, regarded me with undisguised disgust. She asked me what I wanted. I ignored her.

I examined the papers instead. There was the Fort Myers rag, the *News-Press*. They also had one copy left of the previous day's *USA Today* and a few copies of the *New York Times*, also from the day before. "WHY?" the gargantuan headline on the front page of *USA Today* screamed: "Over one hundred dead, hundreds hurt in Portland YWCA massacre."

The *New York Times* offered what you'd expect — restrained prose, no adjectives, and the national angle: "President denounces Portland bombing; scores killed or missing, approximately 300 injured." Their story recounted what the authorities knew, which it seemed wasn't much. Identification of the bodies was also proving difficult. I shuddered a bit.

All the papers had run similar photos: just a pile of brick and rubble where the YWCA had been; twisted rebar reaching up to the flat Portland sky like a witch's fingers; the blackened, burnt-out shells of cars covered in dust and bits of brick. One photo, on the front of the Fort Myers paper, showed a sidewalk with maybe a dozen bouquets of flowers on it. I hurried back outside and into the blinding sun, shivering.

Back in the phone booth, I dialed the number for my dad's office at the naval base in Kittery. He picked up right away. "Kurt," he said, his voice sounding concerned. "Kurt, your mother told me your friend Eddie is missing. Is that true?"

I didn't want to cry, so I bit my lip. "Yeah," I said to him, wishing I was high for the millionth time. "X called and told me they think Eddie and his girlfriend were there for an appointment. They ..." I trailed off.

"Oh ... I'm so sorry, son. I didn't know." There was a pause, and I figured he was trying to think of something profound to say. Instead he said, "The bombing ... it's ... it's just so ... so terrible. It's just beyond description. My god, who could kill children like that?"

I stiffened. *Children?* I hadn't seen anything about that in the papers. "There were *kids, too*, Dad?" My voice croaked. A junkie Lazarus.

"Yes." His voice was thick. "There was a daycare there."

My options at that point were to either return to Motel Shithole and crawl back into the heroin cocoon or get as straight as I could and get my stuff and me across the causeway and to the airport for my flight back to Portland.

Surprising even myself, I opted for Portland.

APRIL 14

Driving up and down their turnpike, smiling up at their cameras, it was like running my finger along the taut belly of the snake. But the snake didn't even notice, David. It didn't strike back. It continued to consume its own tail.

Are they truly this incompetent, Mr. Dennison?

I was ready to be stopped and detained. I was ready for my close-up, you might say. But the succubus, the gorgon, remained preoccupied with itself. I should have expected that.

She is the bard's Queen Margaret, rubbing her hands with the blood of a boy, just as she orders the beheading of the boy's father. She is Satan's bride.

The manuscript is mostly complete, ready to be shared. But they didn't catch me, so I will stay here in the woods, and I will finish it. It will be addressed to you, for reasons you can guess at.

There's still time. For weeks, they'll be busy building their funeral pyre, the one that reaches to the blackened sky.

I did that.

APRIL 15

Robert Frost wrote about his great affection for the woods, about how they were lovely and dark and deep. They are. That is why I love them, David.

I prefer them because they are pathless and lonely, like Lord Byron said. I choose them, because of their melancholy and the patches of grace scattered between the trees. I love the broken sorrow of some fallen birch. I want to live a deliberative life. If I do not learn what the forest has to teach me, like someone once said, then I will have never lived.

So, I am here, in a world where I can breathe, and where I can see with the eyes of a newborn. My lungs are full of the sweet stillness of the air. I will lose the woods, eventually, but not before I grind America's face into the ashes of their narrow, soulless, stillborn lives.

I am hunched over this page, sweating, and I am savoring the woods — the only true place for the few remaining men.

CHAPTER 5

The Hot Nasties' practice space — before, during, and after the Stiff Records deal and their too-brief flirtation with punk rock fame — was the basement of a second-hand record shop in downtown Portland called Sound Swap.

It wasn't much to look at. It had a too-low ceiling, dirt floor, dirty brick walls, and a broken-down couch propped up against a post. The acoustics sucked, too, and the electrical system periodically whipped jolts of electricity through the crappy old microphones and straight into whoever was foolish enough to get too close to them.

Present that day was half of the Hot Nasties — lead guitarist Sam Shiller and bassist Luke Macdonald. The Punk Rock Virgins had come, too — lead singer and guitarist Patti, bassist Sister Betty, and the Virgins' drummer, Leah Yeomanson. Also there was Mike, the big biker who worked as a bouncer at the bar that was the mecca of the

Portland punk scene, Gary's. Mike had been the bands' security guy, van driver, and occasional roadie.

X, of course, was there, too. X was the *human* center of the Portland punk scene.

X had called around and quietly suggested to everyone that the X Gang needed to gather in the basement at Sound Swap to talk about what had happened. To talk about Eddie and Nagamo.

Luke had brought along a case of Bud, and everyone except X had grabbed one — X drank cola, never booze.

It was Sam who spoke first. "Are we sure that they were even there, X?"

X was sitting on the basement steps, looking down at the tops of his Converse. "Yeah," he said. "It's been three days, and still no word from them. Plus, that's where she told Patti they were going."

Patti, sitting on the crappy old couch beside Mike and Betty, started to cry again. Her eyes were red and puffy from crying so much. Betty put an arm around her. Mike reached a big arm across and patted her back. "It's not your fault, kid."

Patti covered her face with her hands and let loose these deep, raw sobs that sounded like they were being twisted out of her guts. "It is," she said. "It fucking is. I told them to go there."

It was quiet again, except for the sound of Patti weeping.

Luke, sitting on Eddie's drum stool, wanted to change the subject. "X, man, what can we do?"

X looked at Luke, his face expressionless. "Not much. The cops told me it's a recovery. No rescue. They say it could go on for weeks, maybe months.... They don't expect to find any more survivors."

They all let that soak in.

"How are Eddie's parents doing?" Leah asked. "Have you talked to them?"

"Tried," X said, looking down. "His mom sounded sedated and his dad didn't say much when he got on the phone. He seemed angry, mostly. I think they're still in denial."

"Has anyone been in touch with Nagamo's family?" Leah asked.

Sister Betty spoke, but it came out like a croak. "Patti and me called yesterday," she said. "They still live at the Six Nations reserve we were at last year outside Toronto.... It was a hard call to make. Brutal, actually."

Patti started to sob again.

"Did the cops say if they have any idea who did it, the ..." Sam's voice trailed off. Nobody wanted to say it: *bombing*. Nobody wanted to say that.

X shook his head, his long hair covering his face. "They wouldn't say. Said they didn't want to speculate."

Everyone had read the papers, however, and there had been no shortage of speculation offered up by "anonymous police sources." In the *Daily Sun*, one nameless cop said they were looking at the possibility it was done by some "far-left radical organization," like the Black Panthers. Another, in the *Press Herald*, had implied it was the work of an agent of a hostile foreign power, like Iran or the Palestine Liberation Organization. One police source, though, had suggested to the Associated Press that there had been a single witness, a security guard who worked at the Y. And an anonymous FBI source was suggesting that someone saw a man get out of the rental truck.

"The witness described seeing a tall young white man wearing aviator sunglasses and a dark ball cap. His description matched that of a young man who had earlier rented a van that matched the description in Newport, Vermont," our old nemesis/ally Ron McLeod had written in an Associated Press dispatch. "Police are increasingly of the view that the bomber was not a foreign national. He was Caucasian, the source said, but his motives remain unknown."

The magnitude of the crime was "well known," however; it was being called the biggest peacetime mass murder that had ever happened in the U.S. More than a hundred dead, over three hundred wounded.

"Who the fuck would do this?" Sam asked, not really expecting an answer. "This is the kind of shit that happens in the Middle East. Not here."

Patti had stopped crying, and Sister Betty spoke next. "Kurt is getting in around midnight. Anyone want to come to the airport with us to get him?"

Mike and Leah said they'd go.

X and the two remaining Hot Nasties shook their heads.

CHAPTER 6

The Casco Bay Recovery Center was located on Forest Avenue, just a mile west of where the YWCA had stood.

For a two-block radius around the demolished, charred remains of the Y, Portland police had set up roadblocks, and the forensic teams had descended on the scene to search for evidence and victims — what was left of them, anyway.

Betty told me that on the first day, crowds of people gathered outside the caution tape to watch the forensic teams as they did their gruesome work. But the crowds had drifted away. I guess it just got too fucking depressing.

"Fucking depressing" was a pretty good way of describing my return to my hometown, too. My United flight landed just past midnight, and the sky was pissing down with rain.

My dad and the Upchucks and Mike met me at the arrivals gate. Mike, I assumed, had been brought along to wrestle me into my dad's station wagon in case I tried to bolt or something. As I walked up, none of them smiled, but my dad and the Upchucks hugged me. I didn't ask where X was.

I'd been gone for more than three months. The Hot Nasties had gotten the bad news from Stiff Records just after Christmas, and I had basically freaked. I immediately fucked off to the only place I had been happy as a kid: Sanibel Island, the location of the one and only family holiday where my mother hadn't shrieked at my father all the time. We'd had two great weeks there when I was ten. So, when Stiff dumped us, that's where I went. To wash dishes. To forget. To cultivate an impressive drug habit.

The Casco Bay Recovery Center was so named so it didn't have to call itself what it *really* was: Portland, Maine's first real rehab clinic for junkies and drunks.

To everyone's surprise, I didn't object when my dad told me where they were taking me straight from the airport. I was too tired to fight it. Hearing about the bombing, and about Eddie and Nagamo dying, had left me depleted. I felt older than dirt, at the ripe old age of twenty-one.

We drove in silence, with Sister Betty sitting beside me in the back seat, holding my hand. Mike was on the other side of her. Patti sat up front with my dad.

I only spoke once. "Has anyone heard anything else about Eddie and Nagamo?"

Dad looked at me in the rear-view mirror. "No, Kurt," he said. "They haven't been positively identified yet, even though the FBI told their families that they're considered among the dead."

"Right," I said, turning to watch Portland slip by in the dark outside the window.

Sister Betty tightened her grip on my hand.

I hadn't called home and told any of them that I was doing smack, of course. But they all knew my history. They knew what I was like. X, it turned out, also knew someone who knew someone active in the Fort Myers punk scene. They told him that Kurt Blank hadn't been seen at any punk shows in the area — because, they said, Kurt Blank "was a junkie, washing dishes at some family restaurant over on Sanibel." Speed had been bad enough — but heroin was the hardest hard drug. The next stop was the morgue. So, to rehab I would go.

We drove slowly, because it was dark and the rain was really coming down. When we got to the center, the Upchucks and Mike stayed in the car (apparently, they'd been told not to make a big deal of saying goodbye). Before I got out, Sister Betty kissed me on the forehead, Mike patted my arm, and Patti gave me a worried look. I retrieved my backpack from the trunk as my dad waited. It contained a pair of jeans, a few T-shirts and underwear, and some toiletries. That's it.

Dad and I went inside the lobby, where a fit-looking woman named Paula was waiting for us. She had short, almost military-style hair and a brusque, all-business manner. Behind her, a big guy in a lab coat was sitting on the reception desk holding a clipboard. It was nearly two in the morning.

"Dr. Blank," Paula said, shaking my dad's hand, and then fake-smiling at me. "And this must be Kurt ..."

"It is," Dad said, putting a hand on my shoulder.

Paula extended a hand and I reluctantly shook it. She kept holding my hand, even though I knew it must have felt cold and clammy — a junkie's claw. "Kurt, welcome to the Casco Bay Recovery Center. I understand you just turned twenty-one, is that right?"

I nodded.

The guy in the lab coat stepped forward and handed Paula the clipboard. "Since you're twenty-one, we require your signature on this consent form," she said, extending it to me. "The length of individual rehabilitation programs will vary, Kurt, depending on the type of treatment, but most of our plans are six to twelve weeks in duration. Often, the therapists may feel that an extended stay would be beneficial to the recovery process, but this isn't a hard and fast rule. But we need your consent to get started."

I looked at the blur of words on the page and then glanced over at my dad. For the first time, I noticed that he was visibly bent, like a twig. And his face looked so sad. He looked many years older than he was. He didn't say anything.

"Do you have a pen?" I asked.

After I signed, I disappeared. For the next ten weeks, I would cease to exist. I would vanish.

But not completely.

CHAPTER 7

Thomas M. Jones hid in plain sight.

Being white, male, and unremarkable looking, he knew the best place to hide was where he'd blend in: Maine and New Hampshire. Maine was about ninety-five percent white (in the rural areas, it was closer to one hundred percent). New Hampshire was slightly more diverse — at about ninety-one percent.

But first, he needed to get rid of the stolen Mercury Marquis. There was a remote possibility someone had seen him getting into it a block away from where he'd left the Ford truck, but he doubted it. And he'd made sure to keep to the speed limit. Besides, he'd been seen at the truck rental in Vermont and at the Holiday Inn. Maybe someone could describe him, maybe not. He wasn't worried about that. But, just in case, he'd ditch the Marquis. He wouldn't be found unless he wanted to be.

Jones had left few traces as he moved through life. No Social Security, no driver's license — other than a very convincing fake one — no credit cards, no passport. He'd never voted. He had been to a medical clinic a couple times — once for a broken arm, once for a dog bite — but he'd given a fake name both times and paid in cash. He was like that: a chameleon, able to blend in to every background.

He was also young, only in his early twenties. That's what someone at the truck rental place would tell the FBI. "Boyish" is how they would describe him. "Looked barely out of his teens."

Thomas M. Jones had been home-schooled by his parents, who — amusingly — were progressive hippie-dippy types. The family of three had lived off the grid, like hermits, in rural Vermont — no electricity, no modern appliances, no TV. They grew their own vegetables, hunted for their own meat, pumped their own water, and kept to themselves. His parents had rejected American society because they believed it had rejected the likes of them. It was a warmongering, corporatist state, they told their son, and they deeply despised it. They hated the manifest destiny bullying, they hated the crowded cities, they hated the pollution and the noise, and they hated America's reactionary capitalist politics. So, they'd withdrawn from it all. Thomas had come along in 1960, when his parents were squatting in an abandoned one-room hunter's cabin deep in the woods near North Pond, in central Maine.

But Thomas M. Jones didn't exist, at least not in the way that other Americans did. His parents didn't register his birth with Kennebec County, and they didn't ever take him to the doctor. They objected to drugs and vaccinations, and they always carried with them a well-thumbed copy of the *Merck Manual of Diagnosis and Therapy*. It was all they needed, they believed.

Their son was a quiet boy, intelligent and a prodigious reader. When he was young, his parents brought him used books they'd barter for in town, and he'd read them slowly, savoring them like they were a last meal. Then he'd reread them.

When he got a bit older and could hitch a ride or walk on his own, Thomas would go into town with the only piece of ID he possessed — a library card, made out in his real name — and he'd meander through the stacks at the Brown Memorial Library in Clinton, as happy as could be. Hours later, he'd walk out with a JCPenney bag filled with books.

With one or two exceptions, nobody ever talked to him. No one ever asked him questions, either. He likely wouldn't have said much, even if they had. Thomas M. Jones knew how to blend in, how to remain *unseen*. His parents had taught him to never trust "outsiders," as they called them. They also made him promise never to tell anyone where they lived. It was an easy promise to keep; he had no interest in the outside world. With books, he didn't really *need* the outside world.

There were exceptions, of course. For a while, there was a girl his age. She worked part-time at the library in Clinton, and they'd talk. She had no interest in books —

even though she worked in a library and was continually restocking the shelves — but she was impressed with how much he knew. "You're smarter than any kid I know," she'd told him.

She'd listen to him talk about Kipling, and especially Kipling's poem "The White Man's Burden," with its thrilling stanzas calling on whites to "send forth the best ye breed," and its disdain for "lesser breeds," and describing how slaves were "new-caught, sullen peoples, half-devil and half child." He also adored Kipling's *The Jungle Book*, he told her, with its tales of a boy who lived in the woods and how the indigenous people were worse than animals.

But it was Friedrich Nietzsche who he came to love the most. It was his father who introduced him to the German philosopher at the age of twelve. "If a person wants to obtain a genuine education," Thomas explained to the girl at the library, "they should drop out of school and read a hundred books." His father had handed him a list, handwritten, and he showed it to the girl at the library, wanting to impress her. Then he tendered his library card and started filling up the JCPenney bag again. On the list, he told her, were one hundred of the best books ever written. With this list as his guide, Thomas started to devour Shakespeare, Plato, Shaw, Dostoevsky, Schopenhauer, and — most of all — Nietzsche. For a boy, reading the German philosopher all on his own, without anyone giving him some context about what was printed on the pages, Nietzsche's musings were electrifying.

He nodded his head to Nietzsche's ravings about Jews, who he called "these impudent people [with] their vulgar souls." Jones also loved Nietzsche's proclamation of what he called the "affirmative Aryan religion." That was his religion, too, he reckoned, although he didn't tell the girl at the library that.

It all had a dramatic and intoxicating effect on Thomas. While his parents slept in the next room in their shack in the woods, he'd stay up to five and six in the morning, watching the sun come up and reading Nietzsche, excited about "the Superman" and what Nietzsche called "the will to power."

Every man seeks to dominate, he decided. That, he told himself, was the nature of all higher life. If a man was strong, he concluded, he could not be evil. "Learn to think beyond good and evil," his father said to him once, and he did. Whether a man had used brutality or love to acquire power, it didn't matter to Thomas. Power was an end in itself. After Nietzsche, he started to read up on other powerful men, like Alexander the Great, which led to Napoleon, which led, inevitably, to Adolf Hitler.

Thomas M. Jones removed his ball cap and scratched his head. He hadn't thought about that girl for a long time. *Where had she gone?* he wondered. *Is she alive?* Didn't she feel the way he did, after he revealed his feelings to her?

She'd disappeared one day and never came back to the library. When he summoned the courage to ask the head librarian, she frowned and said the girl had gotten into some trouble and wouldn't be back. That made him sad for a long time.

Thomas M. Jones looked at the cheap Timex on his wrist. He'd kept to the speed limit the whole way, so as not to attract any attention. He went south along the turnpike first, toward the state line dividing Maine and New Hampshire. As he'd neared the toll booth, maybe a dozen police cars screamed past, heading in the opposite direction. They were heading toward Portland, of course.

A minute later, some fire trucks roared past, their lights flashing. Waiting behind a big truck, with another big truck behind him, Jones watched the flashing lights disappear in his rear-view mirror.

Once through the toll booth, he had gotten off the turnpike at Kittery to use the bathroom at one of the factory outlet places. He bought a Coke at a fried clams place, gassed up, then pointed the Marquis north, back toward Portland and Freeport and Canada.

He was enjoying himself.

He drove north, occasionally pulling over to accommodate the police cruisers and fire trucks screaming toward Portland. In the distance, he could make out the column of smoke rising into the blue April sky. He thought it looked like a fist atop a giant blackened arm.

He went north past Portland, past the exits for Brunswick and Lewiston and Augusta and Waterville. Just past Waterville, he went north and west, heading toward a town called Skowhegan. There he gassed up again, then headed along Highway 2 toward the White Mountains. It was a beautiful day, with the sky a blue that went on forever.

He didn't listen to the news. Instead, he played some Wagner on the cassette tape deck. A bit of a cliché, he knew, but he hummed along to the composer's final opera, *Parsifal*, as he headed toward Newry and Berlin. *Parsifal* had been Hitler's favorite, too. He'd read that somewhere.

Errol, his destination, was a little town in Coos County, New Hampshire, with a population of maybe a hundred people. It was north of the mountains, along Route 16 and at the intersection of Route 26.

As he entered the White Mountain National Forest, Thomas M. Jones knew exactly what was going to happen next. He'd eat at Bill's Seafood in Errol, and he'd take his time. He'd sit away from the doors to the place, in a booth with his back to the kitchen, but with a view of the parking lot. He'd pay cash for his meal, as always. Everyone else would be watching the coverage of the bombing on the single TV above the cash, and no one would even notice Thomas M. Jones.

By then it'd be getting dark, and he'd drive to the remote spot he'd scoped out south of Errol many months before. He'd park the Marquis on a small incline alongside the Androscoggin River, at the end of a forgotten dirt road, and wipe down the interior of the car. Just like he'd done with the rental truck, just like he'd done with the hotel room. Just to be safe.

He'd then stand outside the old Marquis and push on the emergency brake with his right foot, and he'd ease the car forward. And then he'd stand there until the Marquis had been completely swallowed up by the black waters of the Androscoggin.

He'd wait a bit, to see if anyone was around. And, when they weren't, Thomas M. Jones would head into the woods to the well-stocked camp he'd set up.

He'd been getting ready for this day for a long time, and he knew what he had to do.

If he wasn't too tired, he figured he might even lie on his bunk, open up *The Patriot Diaries*, and reread the part about the bombing. He practically knew it by heart.

Life imitates art, he'd say to himself, and he'd laugh.

CHAPTER 8

X couldn't get near Bob Cox in his private room at the Mercy Hospital, of course. Nobody in the media could. Cox was on the fourth floor at the Mercy, away from all the other patients, and under round-the-clock guard by two FBI agents, two Portland Police Department uniform officers, and a couple undercover guys from the Cumberland County Sheriff's Office. He practically had his own team of nurses and doctors and even his own shrink, a therapist from the Maine Behavioral Center. The YWCA security guard was the only survivor who had got a look at Thomas M. Jones, the man believed to be the bomber.

Sheila Cox was folding sweaters in the men's department at Sears when the handsome young man with long hair and an earring approached her. "Can I help you?" she asked.

In his tight black jeans, Converse, and rock band T-shirt, X didn't look like he was in the market for a

Sears sweater. He had a black leather jacket under one arm and some sheets of paper in his hand. He fixed his asymmetrical gaze on her. "I apologize, but I'm not here to buy anything."

Sheila Cox smiled a little and returned to folding sweaters. "No apology necessary," she said, "but most people come in here because they want to buy something."

"Mrs. Cox, I'm a USM student. I write for a magazine called *Creem*. And I don't want to upset you ..."

She tensed but didn't walk away. "You're a reporter?" she asked, her disbelief apparent. "Like for a newspaper?"

"Not exactly," he said. "I write columns, opinion stuff, for a rock magazine."

"Are you from here?" she asked. "From Portland?"

"Yes," he said. "Born here, went to school here."

"What high school?" she asked.

"PAHS."

"Ah," Sheila Cox said, smiling a bit. "One of the smart kids. So, what's your name, smart kid?"

He told her, then added, "But my friends call me X."

"X? Is that your pen name?"

"Something like that."

"So, X," she said, "I've been told by the FBI not to talk to anyone about ... well, about what happened to my husband." Her eyes were flashing.

"Two of my friends were killed by the bomb."

She stopped folding sweaters. "I'm very sorry," she said. "Were they ... also young?"

"Yes," he said, looking down. "Around my age — twenty-one."

"I am so sorry," she said.

There was a long silence. X was not the sort of pushy news reporter she'd probably been warned about. He wasn't even taking notes.

"I really need to get back to work, X," she said. "And I don't know how I can help someone who writes for a rock magazine."

"Of course," he said, and then held up the sheets of paper. "But I'd like to show you something, if you don't mind, and then ask you just one question."

"I don't really have time to read anything right now," she said, looking around. "You can ask your one question, I guess. But I won't promise I'll answer it."

"Thank you," he said. "Did your husband tell you what the man he saw in front of the YWCA was wearing?"

She hesitated before answering. "Bob said he just looked, well, totally normal. Jean jacket, jeans, shirt … clean-cut," she said. She nodded, then added, "Oh, and he said the man was wearing a trucker's cap."

X was looking down. "Was there anything on the jean jacket or the cap, Mrs. Cox? Any logos or symbols?"

"Yes," she said, finally. "Bob said his hat had an upside-down sort of peace symbol on it. Isn't that weird, an upside-down peace symbol? Why would anyone be wearing something like that?"

X held up a piece of paper for Mrs. Cox to see. "Does this look like the sort of symbol your husband described seeing, Mrs. Cox?"

"Yes, that looks just like how he described it," she said, nodding.

CHAPTER 9

Special Agent Theresa Laverty held the copy of the May issue of *Creem* like it was a soiled diaper.

Laverty had a model's face and a model's taste in haute couture, and she was exceptionally smart. She had read, then reread, the Non-Conformist News Agency column — the one titled "The New Dark Age." She threw the magazine down on her bed in the dingy hotel room in downtown Portland.

Being a special agent with the FBI, Laverty could be expected to know the real identities of numerous people who used pseudonyms, like the author of the article, and she already knew quite a lot about the young punk who went by the name X. She knew him, and she didn't like him. Not at all.

She also didn't like Portland, Maine, much. She much preferred her modern condo overlooking the Sanibel Causeway, where it was warm and sunny most of the time, and where she could take her yellow Lab, Sloane, for jogs along the beach. Fort Myers was where the FBI field office was located, and it was where Laverty was based. She was one of the bureau's few in-house experts on violent youth subcultures and extremist groups, and she was increasingly in demand. Historically, when economies went down, Laverty knew, the fortunes of Nazis and other white supremacists went up.

In this, the start of the new decade, the economy sucked. The experts called it a recession, brought on by the oil crisis and other events. So, the haters and the hate groups were signing up more recruits than ever. As a result, the Klansmen and the neo-Nazis and the Holocaust deniers and the Hitler freaks were getting more desperate, unemployed people to listen to their homilies of hate. And they were getting more active, too.

Which, some said, led to more radicalized violence and extremism. Which had led to the Portland bombing. Which, in turn, prompted Theresa Laverty to be summoned back to Portland a month after the bombing.

She picked up the magazine and stared again at X's column. It wasn't that he had written things about the bombing that weren't already public knowledge. The fake name used by the bomber, for example, had been leaked to the news media within days of the bombing. The bomber's use of the United Klan's Mobile, Alabama, P.O. box address on the hotel registry had also been leaked. A couple dozen reporters had spent valuable time knocking on doors in Mobile, vainly waiting for someone to speak to them about the local branch of the

Klan. The bomber's use of a common farm fertilizer and diesel fuel hadn't been a secret, either. Everyone had known about that a couple of weeks after the investigation began; the federal government had issued a ban on mass sales of the stuff to dissuade copycats.

It was something else that had caught Laverty's eye when she picked up the magazine on a rack at the Portland airport and read X's article for the first time — something he'd written that she would have thought nobody else knew. Her eyes had widened when they landed on one paragraph and she'd sworn out loud:

> Jones's use of the United Klans of America's Alabama post office box is well known. What isn't as well known, however, is this: the founder of another virulently anti-Semitic and racist hate group — the National Alliance — has written a novel under a pseudonym. Only a couple hundred copies of the obscure book exist; no mainstream book publisher will touch it. The novel tells the story of a Far Right revolution in which the book's neo-Nazi hero fills a rented truck with barrels containing farm fertilizer and diesel fuel. The novel then describes how the bomb is used to kill hundreds of people at a government building in Washington, D.C.

How did X know about that? Had he gotten his hands on a copy of that book? Or was someone talking to him?

As she sat on the bed in the shitty hotel room, still wearing her coat — a rather expensive Thierry Mugler she'd picked up on her last trip to New York — she pondered for a minute, then reached into her purse and extracted an address book. She thumbed through it to the middle and picked up the phone from the bedside table.

Despite being the target of the largest manhunt in the history of the republic, no one knew where the man known as Thomas M. Jones had gone. No one had seen him since the morning of the bombing. No one knew his real name.

The phone rang once, twice, and then Theresa Laverty spoke. "Hello, Mrs. Lank, this is Special Agent Laverty from the FBI," she said, her tone even. "I believe we met once before."

"No, no, Kurt's not in trouble," she said, "not at all. I just need to speak to him and his friend X as soon as possible."

Laverty frowned. "Rehab? Oh, I'm very sorry to hear that, Mrs. Lank. Do you have any idea when it would be possible for me to go see him? I'm in Portland now."

Laverty listened, nodding, then thanked her and hung up. She looked out the window at a partial view of Casco Bay. The water was flat and grey and featureless.

"I hate this place."

X started writing for *Creem* magazine because of me.

Hey, you owe me royalties, man!

It happened just before Stiff dropped us from the label. The legendary Robert Christgau had been in Portland to take in a Hot Nasties show at Gary's and write up a brief profile of the pop-punk quartet that had been signed — improbably, incredibly — to the influential Stiff Records label. During one really boozy afternoon with Christgau at Gary's before a show, I had boasted to *Creem*'s legendary capsule review guy that my best friend X was "a way better fucking writer than anyone at *Creem*."

Behind his owlish glasses, Christgau laughed and said I was full of shit. I said I wasn't. He asked me to send him some of the stuff X had written for our high school paper, which we called the *NCNA* — the *Non-Conformist News Agency*. Christgau had laughed, saying he liked the name.

So, unbeknownst to X, I mailed off a dozen of the best essays he'd written on his old Selectric for the *NCNA*, including one of my all-time favorites, titled "Punks and Hate," about politics and punk rock. It was edgy and angry.

This was the best part:

> The thing to keep in mind about extremism is that, for a lot of people, it all starts with the best of intentions. It's quite gradual. Most people do not set out to find a girl to kick in the face with

a steel-toed boot, as she cowers on a city street, because she opposes racism and couldn't get away fast enough — and most people don't participate in plots to beat into a coma a guy whose only crime is working a low-paying night job in a factory and being black. Most people do not plan on doing those sorts of things, however much they are angry about something, someone. But some do.

When a young person (a punk, let's say) trades in complexity, nuance, and patience for the arrogance and conceit of bumper sticker ideologies and radical, instantaneous change, all helpfully accompanied by a punk rock music soundtrack — well, hell. Fuck democracy, right? You know what's best, so fuck second thoughts, fuck dialogue, fuck everyone else. Just do it, man.

Punk was, and is, about defiance and resistance and self-reliance; it was, and is, anti-authoritarian, youthful, loud, creative, independent, unique. Punk was wonderful, except on those occasions — more than rare, less than frequent — when it wasn't. When it became the apotheosis of extremism and hate. When it actually became worse than the society it was seeking to change.

At the start, everyone got along. Punks were aggressive and unafraid of a good scrap, sure. But in the early days of the scene, in both London and New York, punk attracted a mélange of countercultures — gays, lesbians, Rastafarians, metalheads, and art students — who were all misfits, but who all went to the same shows and danced to the same songs. It was a rainbow coalition of outsiders. Reveling in that, rejoicing in that.

But then, starting in the late 1970s — in both Britain and in North America — organized racism raised its pointed white head in the punk scene. Spurred on by high rates of youth unemployment, and a widespread distrust of prevailing immigration policies, groups on the neo-Nazi and white supremacist fringes started to enjoy a renewal of popularity. And the skinheads flocked to join them — groups as diverse as the Ku Klux Klan and the Aryan Nations.

And the Far Right skins started showing up at punk shows. They started picking fights. And — spurred on by the older Klansmen and neo-Nazi bosses — they got bolder and better organized.

It was a recipe for hate, and it did not take long for the trouble to start.

A week or so later, Christgau called me. "Your friend is pissed off at the right things," he said. "He can also write better than a lot of the professionals I know. Think he'd want to write for us?"

I told Christgau I'd get back to him pronto. As soon as I hung up, I raced over to X's place (he still lived at home with his parents and his little brother and sister) a few blocks away. I could have called, I guess, but I was so excited I wanted to tell him in person.

Creem magazine, you see, was one of the only rock publications we read. *Rolling Stone* was for boring old farts who listened to Fleetwood Mac and shit like that; *Circus* was too often about big-hair arena rock; *Bomp* was awesome, but really hard to get in a place like Portland. *Creem*, however, was the suburban punk rock survival manual, and it was often for sale at the South Portland 7-Eleven where X and I would pick up late-night Coke Slurpees and beef jerky. *Creem* was our bible.

Anyway, I rapped on the door, and after a minute, X answered. He was barefoot, wearing skintight jeans ripped out at the knees and a T-shirt he'd picked up after a Nasties gig in Montreal. It featured a picture of Joe Strummer decked out like a rockabilly rebel. Below Strummer's face, written in big black letters: "GOD."

At the time, X was enrolled in his first year at the University of Southern Maine, taking some general courses, heading toward a journalism degree. I didn't know what he was planning on doing with that — nobody ever knew what X was planning to do, including me, and Patti, his girlfriend. But, at that moment, I was delighted to know something he didn't for once.

"Brother," I said, bent over a bit, catching my breath, "holy Christ, have I got news for you."

He cocked an eyebrow. "Want to come in?"

I laughed. "No, I want to tell you right here on your front step. I want to be able to clearly see your mug, to see if you'll show some emotion about something for the first time ever."

X leaned against the doorframe. "Okay. What is it?"

I told him.

He didn't show any emotion, of course, even after I gave him a half guy-hug. Not even the tiniest of grins. But he did start writing for *Creem* not long after.

He didn't have a title or anything, and Christgau and the other godlike luminaries at *Creem* — Lester Bangs, Richard Meltzer, Nick Tosches — didn't really need him to write reviews of records or shows. So, instead, they got him to write about politics and culture and what was going on in the news. They wanted him to tell *Creem* readers about stuff that was going on in the world, socio-political stuff the magazine didn't often pay a lot of attention to. As such, they called his occasional column "The Non-Conformist News Agency," which was perfect.

"It's by a guy named X," Christgau wrote in the editor's note that first introduced X and the NCNA to *Creem* readers. "None of us know his real name, although someone in payroll probably does. None of us really know where he comes from, or where he is at the moment. He's X, and he's everywhere and nowhere. He's an enigma! He's a mystery! And he's *Creem*'s anonymous chronicler of non-musical happenings. Shocking but true: there's more to life than KISS and Iggy and the Pistols, boys and girls. Pay attention to X. Boy howdy!"

And that's how X came to write for *Creem*. And that's how he came to be assigned to write about the Portland bombing, too, I guess: because he lived in Portland, because non-musical happenings were his beat, and because he knew quite a bit about the haters who were starting to become more and more visible. He was the perfect guy to write about the Portland bombing massacre.

And the Portland bombing was, as X wrote in his first column about the slaughter, "the biggest act of domestic terrorism in the history of the United States of America."

And it had been done, he later told us, by a red-blooded American boy with a particular belief system. But not the belief system everyone was being told about by the newspapers. Not yet, anyway.

CHAPTER 10

In their glossy promotional brochures, the Casco Bay Recovery Center claimed to offer "holistic wellness," "peace and calm," and "total health" — crap like that. But what they really had was routine — grinding, monotonous, bleak routine, day after day after fucking day.

We were woken up at 7:30. Breakfast was at 8:00. "Therapeutic activities" were at 8:30 — a walk in the gardens (if it wasn't raining or too cold). Then there'd be a stupid lecture and discussion at 9:00. Group therapy at 10:00. Then a twenty-minute break — supervised, of course (everything was supervised). More lecture shit at 11:20 and what they called "creative therapy"; then at noon, the *real* therapy — the lineup to get our meds. In my case, that was some methadone, which always made me feel like puking. But not as much as I would if I were going cold turkey, I suppose. Paula, the head Nazi, had told me the first day that I would be given a declining dose of methadone, until I needed no methadone at all. I nodded. So went the methadone theory.

Lunch was at 1:00 p.m. sharp. There was an hour for that, and the food always tasted like burnt sand. More group therapy at 2:00, more "creative therapy" at 3:00 — plus what they called "fitness" and everyone else called "stretching a bit." At 4:15, we did "peer evaluation," which was the most non-routine part of the whole fucking day. Then, at 5:00, we'd gather in a circle and tell "life stories" for half an hour. Sometimes, we'd get to do that in smaller groups or in pairs. Then more meds issued by the hatchet-faced nurses. Then dinner at 6:00.

After that, some of us would be escorted to Alcoholics Anonymous or Narcotics Anonymous meetings elsewhere in Portland. For those who stayed at the center, there'd be "therapeutic assignments," then "therapeutic reading group," and then "informal sharing." Regrettably, the "sharing" never seemed to involve any little baggies full of magical white powder.

But I actually started to look forward to "informal sharing" and "peer evaluation" during the time I spent there. That was because some of that sharing and evaluation was done outside the watchful eyes of *Obersturmführer* Paula and her health underlings. And because I met someone (more on that in a minute).

The AA and NA attendees would slouch back to the center around 9:00 or so, all quiet and defeated, and the nurses would make us line up again for more meds. And then we'd go off to our rooms to read or — they hoped — "meditate and reflect." Lights out was at 11:00.

I had a private room. There were some shared spaces at my little rehab home, but they didn't put me in one. I think they were worried I might be a bad influence on my roommate. They may have been right about that.

My room was painted beige and it was pretty small, what with all the crap they crammed in there — an armoire, matching dresser, bedside table, and a single bed about as comfortable as a strip of suburban gravel driveway. There was also a chair, which we were told was for "meditating and reflecting." But no phone. Phones could lead to "phone calls," which could lead to "discussions with friends" on the outside, which could lead to "bags full of goodness" being taped to a rock and then tossed over the eight-foot brick wall that surrounded the garden out back. There was a tiny TV, up on top of the dresser, but no cable, so it only got two local Portland stations — WGME, the CBS affiliate, and WCSH, the NBC affiliate.

There was a window, up near the ceiling, but it didn't open. I stood on the dresser and tried to open it on the rather difficult Day Two, believe me.

Jessie was in rehab for booze. I was in for drugs. We hit it off. The thing that brought us together was our shared love of loud music. On Day Two, I was wearing a Ramones T-shirt; she was wearing a Motörhead one.

"Hey," I said as we lined up for noontime pill-popping. "My shirt is better than your shirt."

"Go fuck yourself," she said. "Lemmy'd kick Joey's ass."

It was love at first sight.

She was tall and lanky like me. She had long jet-black hair and the wan, hollowed-out look of junkies and boozehounds. Pretty face, though. She could have been a knockout if she wanted. She didn't want to, however. She wore too much mascara and her ears were adorned with a ton of piercings. On one of her spindly arms, she had a tattoo — an ace of spades, of course. At nineteen, she was a couple of years younger than me. She said she came from nowhere in particular — Maine, Vermont, New Hampshire, wherever. Her parents were "hippie-dippy" types who ran an organic farm now, she said, and they drove her fucking crazy. "They love the great outdoors and the call of the wild and all of that shit," she said during one of our "informal sharing" sessions. "I want cities and lots of noise and lights and people. They drove me to drink."

That wasn't the real story, of course — with those of us domiciled at the Casco Bay Recovery Center, it's never just *one* story — but it was all she was prepared to share at the start.

For my part, I told her I was there because of rock 'n' roll. "Had a band, got a record deal, lost the record deal, lost the band." We were hanging out in the garden on Day Three, and I was shivering. She was smoking a Marlboro, unfiltered. "Could there be a more clichéd rock 'n' roll story?"

"Not really," she said, and we both laughed.

Paula, the she-wolf of the center, openly disapproved of me and Jessie hanging out. In my first week, she hauled us into her office, where a big framed portrait of President Ronald Reagan hung on the wall along with a yellow Gadsden flag, the one with a coiled rattlesnake and the words "DON'T TREAD ON ME" below it.

Paula frowned at us. "Kurt," she said. "Jessie."

"Paula," I said. Jessie grinned.

Paula leaned forward, her big man-hands woven together. "Guys, this is serious. We have rules here at the center, rules you agreed to." She held up one of the sign-in sheets that I hadn't bothered to read. Neither had Jessie.

"What rule have we broken, Paula?" I asked.

She gave me a totally fake smile. "None yet," she said, all teeth and gums. "But you're a boy, and she's a girl. Things happen."

This was getting good. "Things?" I asked, crossing my legs and arms. Jessie was grinning more now.

"Things like relationships, Kurt. Which can lead to —"

"Which can lead to rock 'n' roll, which can lead to dancing, which can lead to extramarital sex, you mean?"

Jessie was giggling now.

Paula's toothy smile disappeared. "Kurt, at Casco Bay, we've been doing this for a long time," she said, all serious. "We know from experience that physical intimacy can simply become a substitute for dependency, which can make getting clean a lot harder, even impossible."

I leaned forward and lowered my voice. "So, you're worried we might have *sex*, Paula?"

Paula looked like she wanted to be somewhere else.

"Here's a secret, Paula," I said, almost whispering. "Do you promise to keep a secret?"

"Yes, of course, Kurt," she said, recovering a bit. "Here at Casco Bay, we pride ourselves on complete confidentiality."

"Good," I said. "Because here's the thing, Paula: I'm into boys, not girls."

There was a long silence. Jessie — who to this point hadn't said a single word — leaned forward. "I've got a secret, too," she said. "I'm into girls."

I looked at Jessie, surprised and delighted. "No shit! Really?"

Jessie smiled. "Really."

Paula regarded us, the personification of a word my dad sometimes used: *gobsmacked.*

"Joan Jett," I said. "Super hot, is she not?"

"Oh yes," Jessie said, laughing. "Hot."

Jessie was really laughing now. Turns out, Jessie adored Joan Jett; in fact, after the meeting, she told me she sometimes called herself Jessie Jett. True story.

Paula wasn't laughing, though. She stood up and looked at her watch. "Well, I'm … I'm glad we've cleared this all up. Thanks for coming by, Kurt and Jessie."

Jessie and I stood up. "So, Jessie and I can continue to be informal-sharing time buddies, then?"

"Yes, of course," Paula said quickly, clearly wanting us to leave.

President Reagan smiled back at us as we left.

CHAPTER 11

Special Agent Theresa Laverty glanced over the personnel file on the desk one more time. Like most members of the Portland Police Department, Detective Frank Savoie had been assigned to the bomber case. But, like just most of the Portland cops, he'd been relegated to scut work: knocking on doors in the neighborhood near the bombing site, asking people if they'd seen anything.

There was a knock at the door of the interview room and it opened a crack. The detective peered in the room. Laverty motioned him in, then stood up and extended a hand. Savoie returned her firm handshake.

"I'm FBI special agent Theresa Laverty," she said. She noted the surprised look on the detective's face. She wasn't sure how much he'd been told about this meeting, but it seemed not much. She waved him to a chair. "I've asked the chief if I could meet with you, Detective Savoie, because of your history."

"My history?" Savoie asked suspiciously, taking a seat. He rubbed a tobacco-stained hand over his stubbly face. "What history?"

Laverty took in Savoie's wrinkled shirt, ill-fitting jacket, and tie that looked like it had come from a Dumpster behind a Salvation Army store. After a long pause, she continued. "Detective, I'm based at the FBI field office in Fort Myers," she said. "In Florida."

"I know where Fort Myers is."

She continued, expressionless. "My area of focus, my expertise, is extremist organizations — criminal ones. And, as you have undoubtedly seen in the media, there is speculation that the bomber was in some way associated with the United Klans of America."

"Yeah," Savoie said, shrugging. "So what?"

Laverty eyed him intently. "Detective, what I'm about to tell you is highly classified. Not even your chief of police has been briefed. And I would like to stress that it must remain completely between us ... agreed?"

Savoie didn't look at all impressed that someone from the FBI was about to relate something to him that was top secret. To accentuate this, he grunted. "So, why tell me?"

"My understanding is that you worked on a case involving Far Right extremists here about three years ago."

"Yeah," Savoie said, his features leaden, betraying nothing. "So?"

"So," Laverty said, "I've been assigned by my superiors to pursue that angle here. We believe ..." She paused. "*I believe* that the Klan had nothing to do with the bombing."

Savoie slouched in his chair, thick fingers drumming on the interview room table. He frowned. "And why do you think that?"

"Two reasons," Laverty said. "One, it's far too obvious. Given our total inability to find out anything about our suspect, it seems unlikely that he would so helpfully provide us with the mailing address of a Klan branch in Alabama if it were of any use to us."

"Sure," Savoie said, "but that hasn't stopped a whole lot of your special agents from chasing their tails down in Alabama, has it?" He said "special agents" with a trace of a sneer.

He was right: the Klan thing was a red herring. "We have to chase every conceivable lead, Detective. We have no choice. Just like the Portland Police Department."

Savoie nodded.

"Detective Savoie," Laverty continued, measuring each word carefully, "I have a theory about the bomber's philosophy, about his belief system."

"His philosophy? There's a fucking philosophy behind killing thirty kids in a daycare?"

Laverty let the comment go. "The bomber was motivated, I believe, by a book. A novel." She watched Savoie's face. "It's a very obscure book, but one that may be about to become much better known."

She reached down and extracted a magazine from her bag and placed it on the table. She pointed at the magazine, which advertised "Heavy Metal Guitar Heroes" on the cover. "Detective, are you familiar with a young man, a local kid, who calls himself X?"

Savoie sat back, his face betraying actual emotion for the first time. "For fuck sakes!" he bellowed. "Don't tell me that little bastard is somehow involved in this!"

Laverty looked as unhappy as Savoie. "I'm afraid the little bastard is. He knows … or says he knows … certain details he shouldn't. And that could create all kinds of problems.… I need your help."

CHAPTER 12

Thomas M. Jones was meticulous. He had everything he needed, and everything was in its place.

He had a four-person L.L. Bean trail tent with a green fly, floor and side walls, and a tan roof. The tent's colors made it almost impossible for anyone to see Jones's secret camp in the woods — not that anyone else had ever come near it. The nearest human was at least a couple miles away.

It was nighttime, but Jones wasn't inside the tent. The New Hampshire woods were unseasonably warm, so he decided to stretch out on his L.L. Bean North Woods sleeping bag, which he had placed on top of a Bean's folding cot. All of the L.L. Bean gear had been stolen by Jones, months earlier, from a summer home in Mother's Beach, outside Kennebunkport. The place was owned by some rich Canadians. They wouldn't even notice the break-in, and the missing camping gear, until they returned to open up in June.

The camp was about an hour's walk east of the spot where Jones had submerged the stolen Mercury in the Androscoggin River. He looked around, his eyes having adjusted to the dark: there was the tent, the fire pit, and a folding canvas chair where Jones would sit and read. There were two Coleman coolers, buried in the dirt, to keep food from going bad. And he'd brought along lots of books, as usual.

He looked around the camp perimeter. To one side was an outcropping of rock, then the small clearing where he'd pitched the tent, then a wall of pine trees. After walking around the area for almost an hour, Jones had located the ideal spot for the tent — a flat, dry patch covered with a bed of pine needles.

Having grown up in the woods, Jones knew enough to place the tent in a spot where he would have a natural windbreak. Wind could make a tent a lot colder at night and rattle the flaps, resulting in plenty of noise. So, Jones had also positioned the tent under the branches of an enormous pine. In that way, the tent would be in the shade for much of the day. Jones knew that a tent placed in direct sunlight could become positively sauna-like in no time. He also wanted to avoid the camp being spotted by anyone in a plane or helicopter.

Details, details.

There was a stream a few hundred paces to the east, but he'd been careful not to set up any closer than that. In the spring, seasonal rains could lead to flash flooding, which could wash away a camp. The soil could also get marshy, attracting lots of blackflies and mosquitoes. In the months of April and May, water could draw wild turkeys, too — which might attract hunters. So, Thomas M. Jones knew to always avoid setting up camp too close to bodies of water.

Between the rock wall and the tent entrance, Jones had built a fire pit. That way, heat would be directed back into the tent on the cooler nights, and the fire would be less likely to be seen by prying eyes.

At the moment, however, no one else was around, and it was quite warm. That was why Jones had pulled the cot outside, so he didn't have anything obscuring his view of the sky — it put him at ease. Wearing just cabin socks, a pair of Dickies cargo pants, and his favorite T-shirt, the Portland bomber stretched out, looking up at the stars.

On the front of the T-shirt was someone's hand-drawn graphic of Friedrich Nietzsche, complete with the philosopher's famous bushy moustache. Below it, Nietzsche's equally famous maxim: "THAT WHICH DOES NOT KILL US MAKES US STRONGER."

He put his hands behind his head and listened to the sounds of the woods.

There was a shortwave radio in the tent, but Jones didn't bother to turn it on. He'd listened to it at various times during the day, and the reports offered nothing new: there were grim recitations of the number of dead, the number of wounded, and the requisite audio clips of the police insisting that they were chasing multiple leads in many states and countries, all of which would soon lead them to the killer or killers. But Thomas M. Jones knew that part, at least, was a lie. He knew the cops didn't have the slightest inkling who he was or where he was. He'd covered his tracks too well. Thinking about it, Jones laughed out loud, amused by their incompetence.

It wasn't like they couldn't have caught him, either. On the day of the bombing, in fact, his journey had taken him south, then north on the Maine turnpike — passing through multiple toll booths, no less. He had stopped to get gas and to pee a couple times at roadside rest stops. He had made no effort to avoid the security cameras positioned above the toll booth laneways. At one of them, he had even looked up and flashed a toothy grin.

Despite all that, nobody had looked twice at him, much less said anything to him. They were all glued to news bulletins emanating from their transistor radios, or looking at the shocking images on TV, with the same clips being shown over and over. He'd slipped by them like a ghost. He *was* a ghost.

The Portland bomber deeply loved the woods. To him, it was home. It was the only place where he had ever felt safe, and where the noise and the clamor and the venality of "civilization" couldn't reach him. He despised cities. He had acquired that, at least, from his parents. In the abandoned huts and cabins in which he had grown up — in Maine and New Hampshire mostly — Jones's parents had certainly encouraged their son to oppose modernity like they did. They rejected the outside world, as they called it, because it wasn't progressive enough.

Thomas M. Jones, however, hated it for an entirely different reason. He hated it because it was *too* progressive.

The woods, meanwhile, were orderly and logical. Everything had a purpose. Every living thing, no matter how small, had a role to play. Nothing was there without a purpose. Everything, as Nietzsche had decreed, was simply there to be dominated — caught, killed, eaten, used — by powerful men. Like Thomas M. Jones was, and like he always intended to be.

By the age of ten, Jones had concluded there was a hierarchy of power, and it was inviolate. It was not to be questioned. Everything that existed, existed to serve the purpose of the Superman — him, and those like him.

His mother had seen this in her son before his father did, and he knew it had worried her. "Everyone is equal," she'd say, insistent. "No one is better than anyone else."

"Then why did you and father move away from everyone else?"

"Because we disagreed with the choices they'd made," she told him. "Not because we thought we were better than them. We just wanted to live a different life, a better life." She reached out and touched his arm. "With you."

He'd pulled his arm away. "I don't like the outsiders," he said, his little jaw set. He crossed his skinny arms. "I think we *are* better than them."

She looked at him with that pained look, the one that he hated the most. The *weak* look, the one he associated with women.

That was around the time that he started to form his opinion about the order of things, as he and his parents squatted in a one-room shed deep in the woods in northern Maine. That was when things started to change for him.

Even now, eleven years later, he could feel the anger rising in him like a fever.

APRIL 25

Mr. Dennison: Out here at the edge of the woods — where I am free in the tearing wind, where I am exempt from your rules beneath a familiar sky — there is a design at work. Not God's design. God is dead, if God ever existed.

The design is plain as the bark on a birch, alone in a stand of pine and spruce and white cedar. And it is there in the echo of a loon's call, deep in the night. And in the swoop of the broad-winged hawk circling overhead. The dominant alpha wolf watching you from river's edge, warning you. The bear heading toward its next meal, hulking, massive, unafraid.

In all of it: strength is the constant. Only the strong survive here.

Without strength, everything will perish.

CHAPTER 13

I kept up with what was going on at home and with the gang as much as I could from rehab. We had access to all the local papers but were only allowed a limited amount of phone calls and no visitors.

It seemed as if the bombing had pitched Portland into deep shadow, everything grinding, airless, and bleak. Reading about it made it hard to breathe some days. Everyone seemed to know someone who had been hurt or killed. Everyone had been affected in some way. Day after day, the *Portland Press Herald* printed grim profiles of the victims. The ones about the kids were the worst. Some had been only two or three years old; they hadn't lived long enough to fill up the assigned biographical space, so there'd be stuff about how "her smile would light up every room" or "he was an angel, and now he is with the other angels in Heaven." It was beyond horrible.

For weeks, the radio and TV news aired similarly upsetting reports: The widower of a YWCA volunteer forced to explain her absence to their three young kids. Or the physiotherapist, hired to help people with disabilities who had been on the job at the Y for only a week. The vets who got together at Michael's in downtown Portland to remember their fellow serviceman, killed while picking up his veterans benefit check. Think of it: a veteran got killed by a bomb in his hometown after having escaped death in the jungles of Vietnam.

Nobody had done a profile of either Eddie Igglesden or Nagamo yet. Not really. Their names had shown up on an early list — "Missing and feared dead," the *Press Herald* headline read — but that was it. The media didn't seem to care all that much about two dead punks, I guess.

But we did. So, X and the members of the Punk Rock Virgins decided to put on a show to pay tribute to our friends. Bangor's Mild Chaps and the Sturgeons said they'd play, too. A cousin of the drummer in the Sturgeons had run the Portland African-American Resources Center on the old Y's third floor and was among the dead.

Gary's was still the scabby, safety-pinned heart of the Portland punk rock scene, so it made sense for the gig to happen there. There'd be no cover, just a raucous, rollicking punk rock wake to celebrate our friends.

There was no way the Hot Nasties could play, of course. Our drummer was dead, and I was still in rehab. So, the Punk Rock Virgins — the feminist punk trio made up of Patti, Sister Betty, and Leah Yeomanson —

kind of stepped up to become Portland's punk voice. "Eddie and Nagamo need to be remembered, too," Sister Betty told me one day on the phone. "They were family."

I told her it was killing me that I couldn't be there.

When Agent Theresa Laverty arrived at Gary's on the day of the gig, she saw X helping one of the punk girls to put up a big picture of their deceased friends on the wall above the drum kit. The photo showed the couple smiling, arms around each other, as they stood at the bar where they'd met.

With Laverty was Portland police detective Frank Savoie, along with recently installed local police chief Richard Chow. None of them were very happy to be back at Gary's. The three approached the stage.

When he saw them approaching, X jumped down off the stage and crossed his arms, like he expected a fight.

The chief stepped forward, smiling, and extended a hand. After a long pause, X took it.

"Mr. X," Chow said. "Nice to see you again. How are you?"

"Fine."

"Good, good," he said, then turned to acknowledge Laverty and Savoie, who were now standing behind him. "I think you remember Detective Savoie and Special Agent Laverty?"

X nodded.

Laverty glared at X and noticed that Savoie looked like he wanted to pull out his service revolver and shoot the assembled punks, X in particular.

Chow, though, kept smiling. "I was hoping we could speak to you, confidentially, about a case we're working on."

"Confidentially?" the girl said, crossing her arms over her "FUCK THE PATRIARCHY" T-shirt.

"Yes," the chief said. "*Confidentially.* Portland PD, for which I am responsible, is working co-operatively with the FBI on ..." He hesitated.

"Finding the bomber you haven't caught yet?" the girl said angrily.

Laverty felt her face flush and heard Savoie swear under his breath.

But Chow was undeterred. "Yes," he said to the girl. "Patti, isn't it?"

The girl continued to glare at them.

The chief turned back to X and pointed at the photo on the wall above the drum kit. "We have a shared interest in bringing the bomber or bombers to justice, I believe. That's why we want to speak with you."

X looked at Chow, as if considering. "Not with those two," he said finally, pointing at Laverty and Savoie. "And anything you have to say, you can say in front of my friends."

Chow's smile slipped for the first time.

"I told you this was a waste of time," Savoie growled. He turned and stalked out of the bar.

"Well," a clearly unhappy Chief Chow said, as he and Laverty watched Savoie disappear through Gary's main doors, "perhaps we can meet on another occasion, X?"

He shook X's hand again, and he and Laverty turned and left.

APRIL 18

This morning, David, I spotted a beaver at work at a tributary off the Androscoggin.

The river is cleaner than it was a decade ago, so the fish and wildlife are coming back. Thus the beaver.

The spot was a rushing creek, and the beaver's dipping back was silver in the sun, spinning sanctuary out of the wood. Dunking beneath the rippling surface, always at work.

It wasn't a dam, I realized. It was an act of defiance, hauled out of the woods and built by the beaver, bit by bit.

That is me, David. I am not building a dam to provide for my family. They're all gone now.

I'm building to stop the river, and to kill every living thing that lies below it.

CHAPTER 14

Portland PD's grey, boxy headquarters on Middle Street was an abomination. It looked like a Soviet-style gulag, thought Agent Laverty.

She sat in a chair across from Chief Chow, who sat behind his huge desk. X slouched in the chair beside her. Following the unsuccessful encounter at Gary's, Chow had decided to try again. He'd called X at home, and more or less pleaded with him to give them another chance. Laverty was surprised he'd showed up.

Detective Savoie had been asked to stay away from the meeting, and he'd been more than happy to do so. "Fuck that arrogant little shithead," he'd said.

Chief Chow began. "X, thank you for agreeing to come in. You don't mind if I still call you X, do you?"

X shrugged.

"Good. X it is," he said, smiling. "Do you know that, to Americans, the symbol X sometimes means yes, but to us Chinese, it always means no?"

"No," X said, deadpan.

Laverty couldn't disguise a grin.

"Okay," he said. "So, X, I must ask: Do you regard yourself as a member of the media? Or as a student at USM?"

"I'm a journalist," X said, his voice even. "With all that entails … constitutionally."

The chief laughed and clapped his hands. "I win the bet!" he said, looking delighted. "I told Agent Laverty you would assert your First Amendment rights in the first five minutes of our meeting! She wasn't so sure."

Laverty seethed.

Small talk over, Chow became more serious. "So, then, let's discuss this." He held up a copy of *Creem*, the one with X's column in it.

"We're interested in some of the conclusions you reached," Laverty said, sitting forward. "We'd like to discuss that."

"You and I are both all too aware of the way in which this department has failed you and your friends in the past," said Chow. "And I think you know that I was recently promoted to chief to demonstrate our commitment to equality and our opposition to extremism."

"So?"

"So, X, I do not expect you to love us," Chow said, leaning forward, "but I think you know you can trust *me*, at least. Yes?"

X shrugged again.

"I do not expect you to name your sources or act as an agent of the police. I am not asking that, and I *will not* ask that of you," Chow said. "But it has been several weeks since the bombing, and we are no closer to identifying a suspect or suspects."

"I'm aware."

"And it is apparent to some of us — me, Agent Laverty, even Detective Savoie — that you have learned quite a bit about these extremist organizations and the threat they pose. So, it seems we have some shared interests. We have a joint interest in catching the killer, do we not?"

X remained silent.

Agent Laverty erupted. "Don't you get it? This monster killed two of your friends! We want to get him. Come on, you aren't even a real journalist — you write a column for a rock 'n' roll magazine, you —"

X turned to look at her, stopping her in mid-thought. After a long pause, he said just two words.

CHAPTER 15

Patti Upchuck waved her arms for the Punk Rock Virgins to stop.

The band had just finished the first number of their set — fittingly, their take on Johnny Thunders's "You Can't Put Your Arms Around a Memory" — and Patti had something to say. Her neon-green Mosrite guitar dangled below her studded belt, the words on the T-shirt she was wearing visible: "TIT SWEAT," it said — the name of Nagamo's band up in Toronto.

The couple hundred or so punks stopped dancing and slamming and went sort of quiet, watching her.

Gary's was packed, typically well over the legal limit for bodies. The Punk Rock Virgins show — which had been opened by the Mild Chaps, and then Maine's only all-black punk outfit, the Sturgeons — was the city's first punk rock gathering since the bombing.

The Virgins and the remaining members of the Hot Nasties, along with X, had gotten together a week earlier in the basement at Sound Swap to plan the gig. The Nasties' Sam Shiller and Luke Macdonald, still reeling from the murder of their drummer and friend Eddie, wondered if it was all too soon. But the Virgins and X wanted to do it. "Everyone else is getting remembered," Sister Betty had said. "We need to remember our friends."

Sam and Luke lacked the energy to argue. So, the show went ahead, and punks were lining up hours before the doors opened. The Portland scene needed punk rock communion — and, of course, charging no cover helped, too.

Patti was standing in the middle of Gary's stage, looking almost stricken, waving her arms. "Oh my god," she finally said, and everyone followed her gaze. In the middle of the pit, edging toward the front, were the three surviving members of Tit Sweat. They'd come down from Toronto. No one had known they were coming, except X, that is, who had set it all up and paid for their train tickets.

When Sister Betty saw the three girls, she started crying. Patti waved for the Toronto band's drummer and two guitarists to come onstage and for the crowd to let them through.

"Everyone," she said, one arm around the shoulders of the tiny but mighty drummer, who had a mohawk haircut and actually *was* Mohawk. "Everyone, these girls are from Tit Sweat, and they've come here all the way from Toronto, Canada."

There was lots of applause and cheering, even though not many of the Portland punks actually knew who Tit Sweat was.

Patti continued, handing her Mosrite to Tit Sweat's guitarist while Sister Betty passed her Danelectro Longhorn to the Canadian band's bassist. "They've lost their sister Nagamo, who was their lead singer, and who was with our brother Eddie Igglesden when he died in the bombing." She paused before continuing, her voice cracking, "That goddamn bomber, tying us up and holding us down."

Tying us up, holding us down.

The cheering and clapping had stopped again, because no one really knew how to react to what Patti had said. There was ten seconds of nothing. Then one of the guys in the Sturgeons, at the back, had the perfect idea, the perfect response to Patti's words: "Oh bondage, up yours!"

At that, all of the girls onstage laughed. Patti yelled into the mic, "I can't think of a better song for all of us punk rock girls to play right fucking now!" The punks started to cheer, while Patti conferred with the band members to see if they all knew the chords to X-Ray Spex's glorious feminist punk rock anthem.

They did, apparently: D, C, D, C, G, A, G, A, *ad infinitum.* That's it. Smiling, Patti stepped up to the mic, one fist raised. She screamed, this amazing and defiant scream, "OH BONDAGE, UP YOURS!" And then the two bands launched into one of the messiest — but one of the most singularly flawless — renditions of that song, ever. The assembled punks went crazy, slamming into each other, leaping up and down, dancing on the spot. The walls and the floor seemed to be bending outward, like the place was ready to burst with too much punk rock joy.

At the back of the dance floor, X stood with Sam and Luke, one hand in his pocket, biker jacket slung over his shoulder. Luke and Sam were on either side of him. Sam leaned in to be heard. "Wow," he said, looking like he might actually cry, "bringing the girls down here was pretty fucking awesome, X. It's perfect."

Through the flailing bodies and limbs, X and Sam and Luke could see flashes of the faces of Patti and Sister Betty onstage — and they looked happier than they'd been in a long, long time.

When I heard about the epic gig they'd organized in memory of Eddie and Nagamo, my chest ached. I was so pissed I'd missed it. How I wish I could have been there with my friends as they remembered the two friends we'd lost.

I didn't want to be there because it was a funeral or a wake. Not that. Punk to me is all about the here and now, you know? It's about *the present*. If you're into nostalgia and scrapbooks and reminiscing, it's decidedly not for you. Punk is about being young, angry, and defiantly present in the moment. So, when Sid Vicious died — or later Joy Division's Ian Curtis or the Germs' Darby Crash or the Ruts' Malcolm Owen — we were sad, of course, but we weren't shocked. If you're a punk, you don't expect anything or anyone to last forever, including yourself. We had made a conscious and non-refundable choice to *never* be like the old farts in the Strolling Bones or Dread Zeppelin — no playing three-chord ragers into your sixties. No nostalgia tours. No career retrospectives. We thought all of that corporate shite was worse than being dead.

None of us therefore figured we'd ever be slam-dancing at a Punk Rock Virgins show and simultaneously collecting a pension. Like Jimmy wrote in that Nasties song, "The Secret of Immortality,"

I think that I know why
I don't give up, I'll never die:
Forever doesn't go beyond next week!

But the murders of Eddie and Nagamo, and of those little kids without biographies, and all those other totally innocent people, that hit us all really hard. We were all bent and broken. We were suffused with grief. We couldn't escape from the shadow that hung over Portland.

So, that gig — with the Virgins and Tit Sweat playing their hearts out, playing like their lives depended on it? That night, lives *did* depend on it.

And I fucking missed it.

APRIL 19

With conviction on our side, we need not fear the coming Armageddon. But the present Holocaust — the real Holocaust, not the fictionalized one — must be stopped.

It will be stopped.

It is an issue that has touched my heart, David. It is a terrible, terrible evil. And the facts cannot be denied: we, the true Israelites, are at risk. The white race — and especially the British and northern European segment, as Kipling wrote — are the peoples who God has permitted to receive and spread the Gospel of Jesus Christ, and which have remained relatively free of the Conspiracy's absolute control.

From where does all this evil come? It is a creation of secular humanism, that anti-Christ religion, which is the genesis of World Government, euthanasia, homosexuality, suicide, legalization of drugs, and pornography. All of it.

The smut peddlers, the atheists, the perverts, the seducers of children: these are the ones who are the diabolical forces behind rock music, modern art, and the drug trade.

We despair, but we must not give up the struggle. Never has our Race faced as many challenges as is the case today, Mr. Dennison. We have been manipulated by the purveyors of popular culture to hate ourselves, to hate our western Christian Heritage. This is done with propaganda like the television series Roots, *or the* Holocaust *series. They try to portray us and our ancestors as fools and liars. To prevail, we must be prepared to break through a wall of fabrications to find the truth.*

Past generations have succumbed to these lies. They have allowed two World Wars to destroy the flowers of our Race. Now, through the new Holocaust, they are willing to sacrifice the buds of our Race. They have opened the floodgates of immigration, diluting our blood while slaughtering those of our Race — by the millions.

It must end. It must be stopped.

I, and others, will stop it.

CHAPTER 16

It was late.

Back in his room, the door closed, with only a single desktop lamp on, X reached into his bottom drawer. There, under half a dozen old *Creem* issues and the *NME*, plus a couple never-opened PAHS yearbooks, he found what he was looking for hidden in a white Target bag.

X reached in and extracted the thick stack of mimeographed pages, about four hundred in all. They were bad-quality copies — likely copies of copies of copies. They were stained and dog-eared and held together with elastic bands.

It was well past midnight. The rest of the family had gone to bed hours ago. It was safe, now, to take it out. If his parents knew what it was, they would be very upset. They wouldn't want something like that in the house. X understood why.

The author of *The Patriot Diaries*, the cover page announced, was Andrew McQuirter, founder and leader of the extreme-right National Alliance in West Virginia, a former physics professor and American Nazi Party publicist. But in the neo-Nazi firmament, he didn't achieve anything noteworthy until he wrote the *Diaries*. On the cover was a symbol that resembled an upside-down peace sign.

McQuirter had written the novel to raise funds for the National Alliance and as a recruitment tool. On both counts, *The Patriot Diaries* was wildly successful: mimeographed copies had started to seep out like some foul virus. Copies would be sold or shared at Far Right rallies, gun lobby meetings, and through the mail by groups like the Aryan Nations and the KKK.

The book electrified those it reached within the racist right; it transformed them. The fact that it was almost impossible to find made it even more influential. For many of these people, the book served as a clarion call to battle — the beginning of the white revolution the haters believed was foretold in Scripture.

It was unlike any other racist propaganda ever produced. Most of the pamphlets, booklets, and texts generated by the white nationalist movement, X knew, were monosyllabic crap, rife with spelling errors, non sequiturs, and insane historical revisionism. They claimed to be factual, but they were anything but.

The Patriot Diaries, on the other hand, was written with what could only be described as an uncharacteristic intelligence and style. Even though it was clearly a work of fiction, and everyone knew it, it had the potential to transform a whole generation of racist activists across North America.

The book tells the story, diary-style, of just over two years in the life of John T., a member of an underground racist terrorist group called the Organization. It begins in September 1991, when John T. and two thousand like-minded men and women are fighting something called the Bender Act, which has outlawed the private ownership of guns. The government — or, as John T. calls it, the System — is employing gangs of black people to confiscate weapons. But John T. and his band of outlaws are determined to overthrow the entire System at any cost.

Writes John T.: "Terrible days lay ahead of us. But God's will must be done."

The book describes how the Organization operated in a cell system, made up of "units" whose five or six members are mostly unknown to each other. "Leaderless resistance," John T. calls it, whose particular expertise is the construction of homemade bombs. John T. relates how to find and assemble the materials needed to construct homemade bombs, along with how to store, handle, and use firearms and explosives. He provides a forensic amount of detail about how to source materials for these explosive devices, and how to build them.

With John T.'s help, the Organization plots to bomb the offices of the *Washington Post*, because it believes the press is a willing tool of the "political police." Along the way, John T. murders one of the paper's Jewish editors at his home.

The Organization also murders one of its own members who refuses to murder a priest and a rabbi. It bombs television transmitters. It rains mortars on Congress during a presidential visit, killing hundreds. It shoots a Tel Aviv–bound jetliner out of the sky with a bazooka. It bombs Houston, Atlanta, and Los Angeles, targeting black neighborhoods. It kills three hundred people at a cocktail party at the Israeli Embassy.

X's eyes narrowed as he found what he was looking for: "Today is the day of our greatest victory. Today is the day for which we will be remembered. Today is the day we struck at the head of the snake — the national headquarters of the Jew-infested Federal Bureau of Investigation in Washington, D.C. And, at day's end, seven hundred of their satanic agents were dead." The book goes on to describe how the agents were slain: After weeks of reconnaissance, John T. drives a truck up to the FBI building, parks, and activates a timer. Twenty minutes later, a massive bomb levels the building, killing everyone inside. The bomb contains farm fertilizer and diesel fuel.

CHAPTER 17

"My parents sucked."

It was sharing time, so Jess and I had adjourned to the garden out in the back. Casco Bay was an infernal hellhole, but they had a nice garden. As often as possible, Jess and I hung out there. It helped us forget where we were, however briefly.

Jessie was smoking, as usual, and I was stretched out on one of the benches at the back of the garden. She was walking back and forth, back and forth, fuming and smoking.

"They were fanatics," she said. "They had this fucked-up philosophy about life, and they insisted that I go along with it, whether I agreed with them or not. They refused to listen to anything I had to say." Her parents' entire life philosophy, apparently, was sunshine and granola. That was what Jess called it, too: "sunshine and granola."

No McDonald's, no fast food, no TV, no comic books, no Slurpees, no fast cars, no technology, no popular culture, no rock 'n' roll. "Especially no rock 'n' roll," she said.

"They made me listen to all this fucking sixties shit on their tinny old record player," she told me. "Peter, Paul and Mary, the Mamas and the Papas, Simon and Garfunkel, Joan Baez, Woody Guthrie, early Dylan. Before he discovered the electric guitar, of course, because god forbid that anyone should ever pick up an electric guitar." She frowned, smoking more. "I fucking *hate* early Dylan."

Jess's parents were against modernity, basically. Also on the list of things to be avoided, in their view, was anything that was popular or mass-produced — or in some way bad for you. "Everything that is worthwhile, basically," Jess said.

So, naturally, Jess started eating Big Macs, drinking Coke Slurpees, watching *Happy Days*, and listening to loud rock 'n' roll music as soon as she was able to. She wasn't a punk, but she was a punk in her soul. She was *against* anything that her parents were *for*.

"You sound like a punk," I told her. "Why didn't you become one?"

She shrugged, lighting another Marlboro. "Where I grew up, nobody had ever heard of the Sex Pistols or the Clash or the Ramones or any of that," she said, exhaling. "Nobody. I was living in the middle of nowhere. There was no punk rock in rural New Hampshire or rural Maine. It's a miracle, actually, that I ever got to hear Motörhead."

She first heard Lemmy's nasal howl on her way into the library, where she'd work after school. A couple guys with long hair were sitting in a souped-up Mustang, windows down, and they had something cranked on the cassette deck. "They weren't going to the library. They were waiting for a girl who was older than me. I'd seen them all together before that," Jess said. "But I had sort of kept away, because they were a bit intimidating. Then I heard the tape they were playing."

It was the first Motörhead album, released in 1977, right around the time that punk was showing up in London and New York and, believe it or not, in far-off places like Portland, Maine. Even though the guys in Motörhead had long hair and had come from the traditional rock scene, they were punks in their attitude.

Jess, standing on the sidewalk near her small-town high school, was jolted by what she was hearing. After a couple false starts, she summoned the courage to approach the pair.

"Hey," she said.

"Hey," one of the guys said, without turning down the sonic barrage coming out of the Mustang's speakers. "What's up, little girl?"

Jess ignored the "little girl" remark. She was on a mission. "Um, what's that?" she asked. "What's that music?"

The guys laughed. "That, little girl, isn't music. That's fucking Lemmy and Motörhead. First album, first side, first song. Motörhead."

"Lemmy and Motörhead? That's their name?"

The guy laughed again. "No, just Motörhead," he said. "Lemmy is the lead singer. Motörhead is his band. Fuckin' awesome, eh?"

Jess nodded. "Fucking awesome," she agreed. It was the first time she had ever used the word *fuck* in a sentence. Her parents disapproved of swear words, too.

That same afternoon, she found a copy of *Rolling Stone* at the 7-Eleven. There, in the classifieds at the back, was a tiny ad for Chiswick Records in England. Motörhead's label. The ad listed some of Chiswick's acts: the Damned, the Gorillas, Dr. Feelgood, Johnny Moped, the 101ers — and Motörhead. Jess paid for a money order at the post office the next afternoon and sent it off to Chiswick Records in London.

"I had it sent to the library where I was working, so my parents wouldn't find out," Jess said, smiling at the memory. "The library had a couple of soundproof listening booths for people to listen to records, mainly classical stuff and jazz." She laughed. "I'll bet that's the first time anyone ever played something like that in there."

"So," I said, "you transformed it into a cool library after that?"

"Not really," Jess said, stubbing out the Marlboro. She frowned. "It was still a weird little library. Some weird people hung out there. Lemmy kept me sane, most of the time."

CHAPTER 18

"What a shitshow," Savoie said, surveying the scene.

He was standing by his rusty Oldsmobile when Laverty arrived. She'd called the night before to tell him they needed to attend the Klansmen's march. Savoie had grumbled about the hour-long drive from Portland and the waste of a perfectly good day. Laverty reminded him that policing a Klan rally in Portsmouth was still a lot more interesting than knocking on doors in Portland, asking people in vain if they'd seen anything. He had to agree.

The crowd that had assembled on the New Hampshire side of the Piscataqua River Bridge was made up of around a hundred men, most wearing homemade Klan robes and chanting racial epithets. Traffic had slowed to a crawl on the massive steel bridge, the midpoint of which was the Maine–New Hampshire state line. The Klansmen's intention was to march from the Portsmouth, New Hampshire, side to the Kittery, Maine, side. By doing so, they probably hoped to stir up some shit and attract lots of media attention. They hadn't started marching yet, but already the gathering had attracted a small army of media.

The reporters and photographers were there, naturally, because they can't ever help themselves. There were almost as many journalists, in fact, as there were Klansmen. New Hampshire state troopers had cordoned off a spot for the assembled media horde over by the High Liner fish factory, a fair distance from the bridge and a considerable distance away from the marchers. They snapped photos and shot footage and occasionally yelled questions at the Klansmen, who looked delighted by all the attention.

The state troopers, who were also present in great numbers, looked anxious but not about the media. They were much more concerned about the several hundred protestors and locals who had gathered on both sides of the bridge, most of them on the New Hampshire side.

Laverty knew the march was just a media stunt, a scam conjured up by racist losers — not even worth her time. But the night before, a colleague in the Memphis bureau had called and told her that a "person of interest" had travelled to New Hampshire to participate in the march, and that he was carrying something he shouldn't be. So, she'd called Savoie and told him to meet her there.

"Want to tell me why we needed to pick up some idiot in the middle of this?" Savoie asked, not bothering with hello or good morning. He pointed a tobacco-stained finger in the direction of the Klansmen. "You don't seriously think the bomber, even a stupid one, would show up for this circus, do you?"

"No," she said, gesturing to the troopers gathered behind Savoie, "but we've got a person of interest detained in the mobile command van. A colleague in Memphis said we should probably talk to him."

Laverty turned and strode off toward the state troopers' van. Savoie grunted and followed.

When they reached the vehicle with "COMMAND CENTER" inscribed on the side, Laverty rapped loudly on the door, which was immediately opened by a burly state trooper.

"Hey. Agent Laverty, FBI. This is Detective Savoie from Portland PD." She flashed her ID. "He's with me."

The trooper glanced back inside the van, then turned back to Laverty and Savoie. "You guys want me to stay? He hasn't caused any trouble yet, but —"

Laverty shook her head. "No thanks." Then she raised her voice, loud enough for the man inside to hear. "Besides, we'll happily shoot him if he causes any trouble."

The trooper laughed, handed Laverty a thin file, and stepped outside.

The interior of the van was no bigger than a clothes closet. In the center was a small metal table bolted to the floor and two metal chairs. A fluorescent bulb buzzed overhead. Through the metal walls, they could hear the voices of the cops outside who were using the command center as a base.

"Detective Savoie, meet Tim Reid, the wizard something-something of the United Klans of America." Laverty wasn't even looking at the hulking man who was slouched down in one of the chairs, both hands cuffed to the center of the table. She opened the folder and examined the single sheet inside. "Picked up today for carrying six unregistered firearms — serial numbers scratched off. Not very smart, Mr. Reid."

Tim Reid was a big man, probably well over six feet, and seemingly all muscle. He was balding, almost chinless, and his face was heavily pockmarked. The grimy T-shirt he wore read "WHITE PRIDE." His sunken eyes radiated hate as he glared at her. "I know my fuckin' Second Amendment rights," he said, smirking. "You can't detain me for carrying."

"Actually, we can, and we did," Laverty said. "You're not in Alabama anymore, Mr. Reid. We *can* send you to jail for driving up here with six unregistered Glock seventeens.... So, where'd you get those, anyway? They're prototypes, I do believe — not even on the market yet."

Reid smiled but said nothing.

"Fine by me, Timmy," Laverty said. "But you're going to do some serious time for those Glocks ..." After a very long pause, she sighed and said, "Unless ..."

"Unless what?"

"Well, unless you tell us something we don't already know. And I know you know how it works, Timmy, because you're already someone's CI down there in Alabama, aren't you?"

Reid wasn't smiling anymore. "What? Who told you that?"

"No one, actually," Laverty said. "I just guessed."

"Look, Timmy," she continued, "Detective Savoie and I don't really care about the Glocks. We're working on something else, something much more important."

"The bombing," Reid said.

"Yes, the bombing," Laverty said, leaning against the door. "You don't approve of the bomb, do you, Timmy?"

"Fuck no," Reid said, sounding like he meant it. "That was way too fucking hardcore. It's brought heat down on everyone in the movement."

"So," Savoie said, speaking for the first time, "you help us, we help you, genius."

Reid paused for a long time before he finally began to talk.

X, Sam, and Luke stood in the middle of the Piscataqua Bridge, watching the assembled crowds. Well, X and Sam were watching, anyway. The three of them had been there for a couple hours, directly below the sign that announced that travelers were now leaving New Hampshire and entering Maine.

Luke was keeping busy by repeatedly stepping back forth across the invisible state line.

"Look, I'm in Maine!" Then he'd step back. "Look, I'm in New Hampshire!"

Sam reached over and punched him in the shoulder. "Cut it out, you moron! We're here for an actual fucking reason, remember?"

"You mean you object to free and unhindered interstate punk transport?" Luke said, continuing to jump back and forth between the two states.

Sam punched him again.

Luke stopped jumping.

X, who'd been ignoring Luke and Sam, pointed in the direction of the fish factory. "There," he said. He handed Sam the binoculars.

"What is it?" Sam lifted them to his face. Luke leaned over the railing, squinting. Because he was born with ocular albinism, Luke basically couldn't see fuck all. He was pretty much legally blind.

X had called them a couple days earlier, when the *Portland Press Herald* had reported that the Klan was descending on the area for what it called a rally "to promote racial pride." (Their race, of course.)

The Associated Press story, written by the X Gang's longtime nemesis/raconteur, Ron McLeod, made it clear that the governors, the mayors of Portsmouth and Kittery, and just about every police agency operating in the two states were very unhappy about the planned march. Portland, and all of Maine, had gone through plenty already, the mayor of Kittery told Ron McLeod, and "none of us need these bigots and troublemakers in our community, stirring up division."

The story concluded with a brief discussion of the unsuccessful efforts of Portsmouth's mayor to get a court order banning the Klansmen from gathering. The move was opposed by the civil liberties people, naturally, because throwing gasoline on a raging fire was apparently encouraged by the First Amendment and favored by the civil libertarians.

When he called Sam and Luke, X told them he wanted to observe the rally and the counter-protest for a column he was writing for *Creem*. But he hadn't told them the whole story.

"That FBI agent, Laverty," X said, his voice low, "she went into that police trailer over there with Savoie."

"The Portland cop?" Sam asked. He scanned the area with the binoculars. "Why do they care about a Klan rally? I thought they were supposed to be out looking for the bomber."

"They are," he said. "That's why they're here."

Sam handed the binoculars back to X, who trained them on the troopers' command post.

"Why would they be here? Isn't this kind of the last place the bomber would want to be, with reporters and cops everywhere?" Sam asked.

"The bomber isn't here," X said.

"So, why are Savoie and the FBI agent here? And why are we here, for that matter?"

X pointed in the direction of the trailer again and handed Sam back the binoculars. "There's someone in there we need to get to."

"Savoie and Laverty just came out," Sam said. "And there's some big fucker with them."

X grabbed the binoculars back and watched as Tim Reid stepped out onto the road, rubbing his wrists.

CHAPTER 19

At Casco Bay, plenty of effort went into preventing any of us from hearing about what was happening in the outside world. Current events tended to be bad or sad, or both, and could result in relapses, you see.

Jessie said that Paula and her platoon of rehab robots treated us like "mushrooms." "They keep us in the dark and feed us bullshit, and they think we'll thrive."

I laughed at that one: mushrooms — that's us.

Inevitably, of course, we'd hear about stuff. We'd learn about things that were a big deal — like, say, the total inability of the cops to find out who slaughtered more than a hundred men, women, and children in downtown Portland. Or, say, a hundred white supremacists holding a rally near the main bridge into Maine, and counter-protestors showing up, intent on killing them with their bare hands, a few dozen cops in between trying to prevent a riot.

Jessie and I heard about it, and we were talking about it.

"Wish to fuck I had been there," I said as we huddled on the floor in a corner of the common room. "We'd kick some Nazi heads."

Jessie regarded me, eyebrow up. "Not a peace and love kind of queer boy, are you? You and your buddy X get into a lot of fights?"

"All the fucking time," I said. "We almost never start fights, but we usually finish them. You have to understand, in the early days of the scene, it was pretty great. Really diverse. Gay kids, overweight kids, quirky kids, arty kids, minority kids. Lots of freaks and geeks. It was good. Everyone got along. There were even skinheads, but none of them were racist back then. We'd rarely have any problems at our shows — except from the cops, of course."

"If everyone got along so well, why'd you get into so many fights?"

I shrugged. "The scene got bigger. We'd get hundreds of kids showing up at a community hall gig, just by word of mouth. And people started to show up who we didn't know." I shook my head. "Even some of the jocks who hated us in high school started coming. They'd shaved off their hair and were into hardcore and straight edge shit, and they'd come to the shows looking for a fight."

"So, you'd give them one?"

"Fucking right we would," I said, a bit defiantly. "Nobody messes with our friends."

Jessie smiled. "Kurt Blank, defender of oppressed punks." She squeezed my arm. "You're a good guy, you know? So, the racists, how did all that happen? Did they come to your shows, too?"

I scowled. "Sometimes. But if we saw them making fascist salutes or whatever, we'd kick their asses and throw them out."

Jessie looked a bit confused. "But I don't get it," she said. "You punks were queers and minorities and all that. Why would the skinheads want to go to your shows? Why not just stay away?"

I held up two fingers. "One, they would come just to beat us up. It made it easier for them: we were all in one place."

"Okay. What was reason two?"

I squirmed a bit. "It's kind of hard to explain."

"Try me."

I thought for a moment. "We were outsiders, they were outsiders," I said. "We had that in common. Also, in the early days, some punks were pretty careless about racism and anti-Semitism and all that. Siouxsie Sioux would give Nazi salutes at shows. Johnny Rotten had his famous swastika T-shirt. The Ramones had songs with lyrics that seemed to praise the SS and all that shit, even though Joey, the lead singer, was Jewish. Punks weren't all as progressive then as they are now. They weren't as political. Some of them were actually pretty fucking clueless about politics."

"Were you and X always political?"

I nodded. "He was, for sure, right from the start," I said, remembering. "He taught me a lot. Changed the way I thought about a lot of things." I trailed off. "He was really important to me."

"I'd say he still is," she said. "You heard from him since you've been here?"

I shook my head and looked down.

"I knew a guy back when I was younger," she said. "A bit like X, in that he was the first kid my age who seemed to care about ideas. He'd come around where I worked and talk my ear off about politics, philosophy, books."

"What kind of politics?"

"Oh, nothing like yours and X's," she said, stretching her long legs out in front of her. "He was smart, but he was really, really conservative. I got to not like most of his opinions, actually, especially his views on women."

"What happened to him?" I asked.

"Dunno," she said, looking a bit uncomfortable. "We lost touch, and I was happy to keep it that way." She paused, then abruptly changed the subject. "So, did I ever tell you I know how to play drums?"

"You what?"

CHAPTER 20

The remaining members of the X Gang knew that Eddie Igglesden wasn't alive somewhere. Knew that his body was never going to be found. Eddie's parents finally accepted that truth about ten weeks after the bombing and commenced the sorrowful work of dealing with the priests at the Cathedral of the Immaculate Conception in Portland — even buying a casket from Jones, Rich and Barnes that would remain empty for the funeral.

Word got around the scene, and even to me at Casco Bay (Sister Betty phoned and told me). I promised I'd do everything I could to be at my drummer's funeral.

Sister Betty also told me that Nagamo's family had held a memorial for her a couple of weeks earlier, at the Six Nations reserve up in Ontario. All the Virgins, along with X and Sam and Luke, had gone. Mike the Biker had driven everyone up there in the old Econoline van we'd toured in when the Nasties were still together.

Eddie's funeral was set for around the time Jessie was supposed to be discharged from Casco Bay. For me, however, it would mean leaving a few days sooner than planned, which was apparently against the rules and which necessitated a meeting with Paula and some of her storm troopers so I could beg for permission to leave early. My dad showed up and pledged to keep an eye on me every minute of every day. And, for my part, I assured the Casco Bay folks that they'd chased the toxins out of my blood and had instilled in me, forever, the Twelve Steps to sobriety: honesty, hope, faith, courage, integrity, willingness to change, humility, discipline and action, forgiveness, acceptance, knowledge and awareness, service and gratitude.

Anyone who knew me, of course, knew that was all basically bullshit. If the Twelve Steps were a junkie's equivalent of the Ten Commandments — well, then I was almost certainly going to be landing back at Casco Bay (or a funeral home) sometime soon. I mean, on a good day, I might be able to pull off forgiveness and knowledge and awareness. But hope, courage, or humility? Not a chance. Not me. But I didn't tell Paula that.

Honesty? That I could do. I'm a fucking champ at honesty — usually far too much of it. And honestly, I was scared shitless. I was scared of returning to the real world, scared of seeing my friends again, scared of going to Eddie's funeral, and scared of seeing X. Scared of *being seen by* X. That I honestly wasn't ready for.

Anyway, Paula wasn't moved by any of my promises. She didn't trust me, and she all but said so. But my dad's pledge to keep an eye on me and ensure that I attend every NA meeting and every post-release checkup swayed her in the end. "We will release him into your care, Dr. Blank," Paula said, clearly skeptical. "Good luck."

After winning my early release, I told Jessie that I was scared I'd relapse. At Casco Bay, she'd become my Mother Confessor, and I confessed that I had fear "in abundance."

"What do you fear?" she said, bemused, shoving T-shirts and jeans into an army surplus duffel bag, preparing for our joint departure.

I shrugged. "Falling off the wagon, which seems inevitable," I said, "and seeing X and the rest of them … seeing their disappointment in me, again."

She cocked an eyebrow. "X is supposed to be your best friend, and you're afraid of seeing him?"

"Not really. Well, sort of," I said, sitting cross-legged on the floor. "I'm not afraid of him. I love him. I like to say he's my brother of another mother, and he is, but …" I tried to think of the right words. "But I just always end up disappointing him, you know? And I hate that. I hate that the most."

"If he is really your best friend, your brother like you say, then he'll forgive you," she said, pausing in her packing. "You've been busting your ass to get clean and get better here, Kurt. This X guy is a total asshole if he doesn't give you credit for that. You deserve a shot at redemption."

She sat down beside me on the floor. Paula and one of her "teams" walked by, looking in at us with concern.

Jessie waited until they were farther down the hall. "Look, I have something to tell you," she said, her voice low. "My folks paid for me to be here. And they'll never say it, but they don't really want me coming back to stay with them. We always fight and shit. So, if you want, I can stay in Portland for a while. You know, keep an eye on you and all that. We can be a sobriety tag team."

"Really? That would be fucking awesome! My dad's based in Kittery, but he's rented me a place in South Portland, near the mall, that has plenty of room. Having you there would mean that he wouldn't need to be there all the time, watching me. I know he'll go for it. He told me he likes you."

"Cool," Jessie said, laying a hand on my arm, right beside my tattoo of Jimmy Cleary's initials, which I'd gotten what felt like a million years ago. "And I can go to the funeral with you, if you want — moral support and all that."

"That'd be awesome, Jessie," I said, ecstatic. I was feeling a lot less anxious about leaving Casco Bay. "Thank you."

"No probs, Point Blank," she said, using my sometime stage-name. "It helps me out, too. It'll be good. For starters, I won't need to run away from my folks again, like I've done a million times."

"When was the first time you ran away?" I asked. "How old were you?"

"Sixteen." Her features had grown dark.

"Did you have a fight with your parents?"

"No," she said. "It was something else. We were living in this tiny shithole town in Maine called Clinton. I was working after school at the town library, reshelving books mainly. There was this kid who used to come in. I mentioned him before. We'd talk all the time — about philosophy, ideas, art. He knew so much stuff, but his ideas were kinda fucked up. They made me uncomfortable, but I was so grateful to be able to talk to someone who had a functioning brain, you know, so I put up with it." She gave a little laugh. "There weren't many functioning brains in Clinton."

I nodded.

"Anyway," she said. "He was interested in me. He said so."

"Did he say he loved you like I do?"

She laughed again. "No, he never said that. He'd never say that. He actually said that love didn't really exist. That it was all just mutual dependence and biology."

"That's kind of depressing."

She nodded. "Yeah, it was. Anyway, I didn't know for sure I was gay back then, but I suspected it. I struggled with it. But I definitely knew I had no physical attraction to him, not at all. But like I said, he was attracted to me." She lowered her voice. "So, he jumped me one night as I was walking home after work. He pulled me into the woods, and … he raped me."

"Oh, shit, Jessie, I'm so sorry. We don't have to talk about this if you don't want to …"

She shook her head. She wasn't crying or anything. She was calm. "It's okay. He wasn't big, but he was pretty strong. Wiry, you know?" She paused. "When he finished, I ran home. I didn't tell my parents. I never went back to the library. I never saw him again. Not long after that, I ran away, first to Boston, then Albany, then a bunch of other places. I just didn't want to see him again. Clinton's a small place."

"Jesus Christ," I said, putting an arm around her and pulling her closer. "I'm so sorry, Jess."

After a few minutes she sat up. She just sat there, staring off in space, looking sadder than I had ever seen her.

"Kurt," she finally said.

"Yeah?"

"I haven't thought about him in years, but lately I haven't been able to *stop* thinking about him. Where he is, what he's doing now, all that. I just sort of suddenly remembered him one day during one of those stupid group therapy sessions we did with Paula. Right out of the blue, I started thinking about him, and something he'd said to me once, when we were in the library."

"What?"

Jessie looked right at me then, and she looked a bit afraid. "It was one of the last times I ever saw him. He'd changed — dressed differently, talked differently. I didn't like him as much anymore. And he said he'd read a book, this super-important book. He told me it had changed him forever."

"What book?"

"I can't remember the title," she said. "I'd just thought it was bullshit at the time. Schoolboy bragging, you know."

"What was it, Jess?"

"He said he was going to do something that would be remembered for a long time." I felt her shiver under my arm. "He said he was going to kill a bunch of women one day for their sins. With a bomb."

MAY 1

Like that Russian dissident said, David: the forest does not weep over one tree.

I am a dissident, like him. And I believe in the grim procession that is man's history, that day in Portland — in and of itself — matters little. No real man weeps over that.

What matters, in the days to come, is that Portland be remembered for what it was: a clarion call. A day when men finally woke up and became men again.

Nietzsche, were he here, would celebrate it. He anticipated my quest. "I am a forest, and a night of dark trees," he wrote. "But he who is not afraid of my darkness, will find banks full of roses under my cypresses."

Darkness lights the way, Mr. Dennison.

CHAPTER 21

"I'm takin' enough of a risk staying in fuckin' Portland and talkin' to a couple cops in a motel room," Tim Reid growled, deeply unhappy. "I need to get back home or my brethren are gonna start wonderin' where I am and start askin' questions."

Theresa Laverty shook her head. "I don't care what your brethren think. You're not going anywhere yet. And you're lucky to be in a motel room and not a jail cell, Mr. Reid."

It was true. He should have been facing a judge on the weapons charge, and probably a few other things, but he was instead in a room at the very rear of the Holiday Inn across from the Portland mall. Chief Richard Chow had agreed to the unusual arrangement to protect Reid's status as a CI — a confidential informant — and to also "facilitate loosening his tongue," as Chow had put it.

But Reid's tongue had not been loosened. Not yet.

Everything he had to say about the Klan so far, Laverty already knew. And anything he had to say about the Portland bombing could have come from the news media. More than once, he'd claimed to know something about the Portland bomber, but he hadn't divulged anything yet. He wanted "garn-tees," he said.

Laverty was getting impatient, but it was Savoie who spoke next. "We said we'd drop the weapons charge. We're giving you a bus ticket home. What the fuck other *guarantees* do you want?"

Reid was on the floor, his back to the hotel's shiny wall. "You're hurtin' my business by keepin' me here," he said. "I need compensation."

"What business, Mr. Reid?" Laverty said. "You supposedly run a private security firm in Mobile. But we know for a fact that you don't have a single client."

Reid shook his head defiantly. "They all got scared away when the FBI started knockin' on every door in town!" He pointed a finger at Laverty. "You guys were chasin' the bomber all over town, and it freaked everyone out! And he wasn't even there. Never was."

"How would you know where he is, Mr. Reid?" Laverty said coolly. "And, for that matter, how are you so sure *who* he is?"

"I'm not sure," Reid said, getting to his feet and walking across the room to his unmade bed. As he sat down, the mattress creaked under his weight. He was big boy. "But I got suspicions."

"What suspicions?" Savoie prodded.

Reid examined his big hands, pondering. "Well, the bombin' was pretty much a carbon copy of the one described in *The Patriot Diaries*," he said, quieter. "Step by fuckin' step."

"We already know that," Laverty said, unimpressed.

Reid looked at her. "Yeah," he said coolly after a long pause. "But there ain't too many copies of the *Diaries* floatin' around."

"We know that, too," Laverty snapped. "So?"

"So," he said. "So, the United Klans of America has its own printin' press, you know."

"We know."

"And we are the only organization that's got approval from McQuirter himself to sell the *Diaries*," he said, head down, even quieter now. "We do a pretty good business sellin' bound copies …"

Laverty's eyes narrowed. She moved across the room and sat on the bed. "You keep track of who buys it?"

He looked amused. "Yep. Only a dozen or so copies sold in Maine and New Hampshire in the past three years or so.… Kept track, y'see."

"Mr. Reid," Laverty said, trying hard to hide her excitement, "we need those names."

Reid reached across to the bedside table and retrieved a pen and some Holiday Inn stationary from the desk. He extended it to Laverty. "Write it down," he said. "Gun charges dropped and a thousand bucks cash."

"Mr. Reid …"

"Two thousand."

Laverty snatched the paper from Reid, pulled her own Mont Blanc pen from her purse, and scribbled out the terms. "There," she said, handing the paper back. "I'll take you to my bank and get you the money personally, right now. But first, give us the names."

Reid stood up slowly and reached around to the rear pocket of his Wranglers. He extracted a folded-up piece of paper that looked like it had been ripped from a ledger and handed it to her. "Had it on me all along," he said, grinning as Laverty and Savoie scanned the handwritten list. "Now, let's go get my money."

Less than an hour later, the two cops dropped Reid back off at the Holiday Inn, told him to leave Portland, then sped off to meet with Chief Richard Chow.

CHAPTER 22

The day of Eddie's funeral was sunny, and the big round stained-glass windows above the main doors at the Church of the Immaculate Conception were glittering with reds and greens and blues. Little bits of colored light were dancing on people's faces inside, and it made me feel a bit better. It was pretty.

When Jessie and my dad and I arrived, the X Gang was already there, except X. Every one of them was wearing black, and they looked pretty miserable. Also present were FBI special agent Laverty and the local cop, Savoie. Lots of people from the Portland punk scene were there, too, along with kids who'd known Eddie at Holy Cross or PAHS. His family and relatives were there, too, of course. They didn't talk much to any of the punk kids.

When Patti and Sister Betty spotted us, they came right over and hugged me and said hi to my dad. Dad said he wanted to go and give his condolences to the Igglesdens and headed toward the front of the church.

"You look great, babe," Sister Betty said. "You've gained weight!"

"Yeah, prison food'll do that to you," I said. I stepped back a little and gestured toward Jessie with a bow. "Patti, Betty, this is my friend Jessie. We met at Casco Bay."

Patti looked a little uncertain, but Sister Betty stepped right up to Jessie. "I wish we were meeting on a happier day," she said, shaking her hand. "But it's great to meet any new friend of Kurt's."

Jessie smiled.

I looked around. "So ..."

Patti shook her head. "He's not here yet. Said he had to meet someone for a column he's writing or something."

"Gotcha," I said. "So ... how is he?"

"He hasn't called you at Casco?" Sister Betty asked.

I shook my head.

"He's X," Patti said, reaching across and squeezing my arm. "You know how he is. Tall, dark, frustratingly mysterious."

I laughed. "Yeah. Sounds like him."

Sister Betty pointed to the big wooden doors of the church. "Speak of the devil."

X was standing just outside the open doors, looking down at one of the little notepads he always carries. He hadn't seen me yet.

"This is going to be interesting," I said, then looked at Sister Betty. "Can you introduce Jessie to everyone while I go talk to him?"

"Sure," she said, taking Jessie by the arm. "Good luck, babe."

I started walking slowly toward X. I hadn't seen him in months — not since Stiff had dropped the Nasties, not since I had taken off for Sanibel Island — but he looked exactly the same. Black Converse, skinny black jeans, black leather jacket, and today a plain black T-shirt. His long, wavy hair hung down, obscuring his face.

"Hey," I said quietly as I walked up.

He looked up and fastened those asymmetrical pupils on me. He didn't smile, and he didn't move. "Hey."

"I just got out. It's a bit early, but ... you know, I needed to be here."

He didn't say anything, and I suddenly felt stupid. I turned to go. "I'm here with my dad and a friend, so —"

"You look better," he said. "*Are* you better?"

I'd been practicing various answers to this question, but none of them would really work with X. He knew me better than anyone. "I'm an addict," I said. "I'll always be an addict. Being better is relative now."

He said nothing for a long time, then nodded his head. "I'm glad you're here, man. We all missed you."

At that, my resolve sort of fell apart and I started to cry. "I missed you guys so fucking much," I said. Then, remembering where I was, "I guess I shouldn't swear on the steps of a church."

He put a hand on my shoulder. "God hears worse," he said. "Let's go find the others."

I gestured at the notebook. "Working on something?"

His voice was low. "The bombing," he said. "I may have something."

I turned to him. "You really need to meet my new friend Jessie then."

X arched an eyebrow. "Why's that?"

"Brother," I said. "She knows who he is."

As I inhaled, I was hit with the smell of sour beer mixed with leftover pizza and human sweat. It was not a pleasant smell, but I'd missed it just the same. I was finally home!

After Eddie's funeral, the Virgins and the remnants of the Hot Nasties — plus X and Jessie and me — reconvened in the practice space in the basement at Sound Swap.

I hadn't been there for a long time, and it was pretty awesome to be back but also sad. The ramshackle drum kit that Leah and Eddie had shared was still over in the corner. It wasn't hard to picture Eddie behind it, wailing away in that Keith Moon style of his.

I explained to Jessie that since high school, it had been our place — our safe Portland punk home. The owner of Sound Swap, an older guy named Steve, had said we could use the basement to practice for a few weeks until we found something else. Four years later, we were still there, churning out three-chord ranters about bad dates, teenage angst, and buying Slurpees at the 7-Eleven. It was where we hung out, jammed, drank beer, smoked dope, and talked about whatever.

At the moment, though, nobody was talking much. There wasn't much to say.

Sam had put the Clash's *London Calling* on a cassette player. "Clampdown" was on low, and nobody was talking. We just sat listening to Strummer's familiar rasp.

I decided to say something, mostly because I can't help myself. "That was rough," I said. "Does anyone know how Eddie's parents are doing?"

Sister Betty shrugged. "Better, I guess," she said. "They seem to have accepted it."

"That sucks," I said.

Sam was watching X, who was quietly flipping through his little black Moleskine notepad. "What's the next column about, X?"

X didn't look up. His long hair hung down over his face. "All this," he said, meaning the bombing and the aftermath.

I cleared my throat. "So, Jessie's a drummer, folks. Comes from the Motörhead side of things, but she's pretty good, I hear."

Jessie, from her spot on the couch, looked mortified. "I am not!" she said, protesting. "I never said I was any good, Kurt! Jesus, you've got a big mouth!"

"I do not," I protested.

Sister Betty and Patti laughed. "Oh, yes he does," Sister Betty said.

"Whatever. But if you can't play an instrument, you're uniquely suited for punk rock," I said. "Three chords, one beat, you're good to go. That's punk."

Sister Betty nodded, smiling. "When Patti and I started, we knew two chords. So, we'd play 'Roadrunner' by the Modern Lovers for half an hour. D, A, D, A. Later, we learned G and started playing 'Gloria' and 'Wild Thing' for hours."

"Nice," Jessie said. "If you're going to know three songs, those are the three to know."

The Upchucks, Leah, and Jessie started talking about shared musical likes and dislikes, with Sam and Luke occasionally contributing, the Clash album playing a bit louder now. Everyone seemed to be feeling better, grateful to have left behind the sadness of the funeral. As they chattered away, I decided to use the opportunity to speak to X.

"Brother," I said, "you need to talk to Jessie. She knows stuff."

X looked at me. "So you said at the church. How?"

I looked at her as she chatted with our friends. "Her parents were hippie counterculture types, living off the grid and all that shit. She lived in small towns and worked after school at a library. That's where she thinks she met him."

"How does she know?"

"The stuff he said to her then, the stuff he did." I looked over at Jessie and lowered my voice to a whisper. "This guy raped her, X. She remembers everything about him."

X looked at Jessie, then back at me. “I’m really sorry to hear that,” he said, his pupils getting dark. “What’s the connection?”

“The things he said to her. He told her he was going to do something dramatic one day. Said he’d read this book, and he was going to blow something up. Fucking crazy shit.”

X was looking at me intently. “Which book?”

“She can’t remember. It wasn’t in the library where she worked, though. He told her it was a banned book or something, from the underground.”

“Was it called *The Patriot Diaries*?”

“I don’t know. You should talk to her.”

“I will.”

I could see that the Virgins and the Nasties liked Jessie. The bunch of them were laughing and smiling, talking about music and about the Clash.

Sister Betty looked up at me. “Hey, Kurt. You up to playing something? Sam and Luke want to jam with Jessie here, see how good she is. You up for that?”

“Fuck, yeah,” I said, clapping my hands, heading down the stairs, “I’m up for that.”

And that’s how Jessie came to drum for the Hot Nasties.

And how X learned the bomber’s name.

CHAPTER 23

"I think we've been going about this all wrong." Detective Savoie sounded unhappy, as usual. Laverty could hear his labored breathing over the phone.

Laverty was in an interview room at the boxlike headquarters of the Portland PD, going through Tim Reid's list again. A half-dozen Portland detectives buzzed around, working the phones. Savoie, meanwhile, was on the road, speeding around southern Maine in his Oldsmobile, a convoy of police following him. They were trying to track down the men — they were *all* men — who had contacted the United Klans of America in Alabama to purchase a copy of *The Patriot Diaries* in the past four years.

Reid's list, however, was out of date. Most of the men had moved or, in at least two cases, had died. Not one still lived at the address indicated on Reid's list.

"Are the names Reid gave us fakes?" Laverty asked.

"Not all of them," Savoie said. He was calling from a pay phone at a Maine turnpike toll booth just north of

Kittery. "We've talked to some neighbors who remember some of these douchebags, but they all say they're long gone or dead. Chasing names on this list ain't working, Laverty."

"Well, we can't give up," she said, looking at a map of Maine and New Hampshire. "This is the first good lead we've gotten in weeks. Hell, it's the *only lead* we've had in weeks."

"I know," Savoie said. "But this guy isn't stupid. I'm willing to bet the bomber is one of the guys who used a P.O. box and an alias."

Laverty looked down at the list, several copies of which were scattered across the table. "Yeah," she said, "there are a lot of P.O. boxes on here."

"Yep."

There was a long pause. "Are we wasting our time, Savoie?"

"I don't think so. But I do think we're going about it the wrong way. I don't think we'll find him just by chasing old names on Reid's list."

"How then?"

"Two things. We know the bomber isn't an old guy. The eyewitnesses say he looked young, almost like a teenager. So, he's more likely to be one of the ones who bought the *Diaries* fairly recently."

"Sure. Of course. And?"

"Reid said ninety-nine percent of the guys buying the book sounded nervous or scared. Like they didn't want to get caught."

"Yeah. So?"

"So, the bomber is in the one percent. He's young, and he didn't wear a mask at the motel, at the Y, or at the truck rental place. It's like he isn't afraid to be ID'd. He drove that truck right up to the YWCA, in broad daylight. There could've been a hundred closed-circuit cameras around, even though there weren't. The security guy, Cox, said he was wearing jeans, jean jacket, a trucker's cap, right?"

"Right."

"No disguise, no nothing," Savoie said. "He was practically daring us to catch him."

Laverty was unconvinced. "Why the Thomas Jones pseudonym then? Why just totally disappear? If he was unafraid, like you say, why not do another bombing?"

Savoie grunted. "I dunno. All I know is he's not afraid, but he also doesn't want to make it easy for us."

"Where are you going with this?" Laverty asked, feeling tired and frustrated. She hadn't slept since Reid gave them the list two days earlier.

"I think he just got in that stolen Marquis and drove away. He observed the speed limit, didn't do anything to attract attention. But he wasn't really hiding, either."

"And?"

"And," Savoie said, "I had the guys go through the tape for one of the toll lanes near Kittery."

"We've looked at all of those tapes before."

"Not all of them. Not the trucks-only lane. We didn't check that." He paused. "Laverty, we've got tape of a young guy driving a Mercury Marquis on the morning of the bombing, going through the trucks-only lane."

"Really?" she said, standing up. Chief Chow stopped what he was doing and walked over to stand beside her.

"And," Savoie said, "he slows down, stops, and pays the toll, and then he does something really fucking weird."

"What?" Laverty said, louder.

"He looks right up at the closed-circuit camera," Savoie said, "and he smiles."

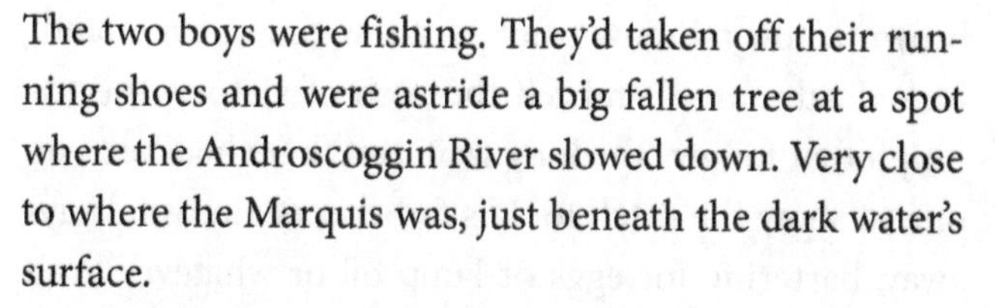

The two boys were fishing. They'd taken off their running shoes and were astride a big fallen tree at a spot where the Androscoggin River slowed down. Very close to where the Marquis was, just beneath the dark water's surface.

Thomas M. Jones took aim.

Through the scope of his stolen rifle — a Winchester Model 70, which he considered the best deer-hunting rifle ever made — Jones could see that the boys were likely in their early teens, having fun and totally oblivious to his presence. He was maybe three hundred feet away from them, hidden in the shadows at the mouth of the woods.

He watched as they chattered away, enjoying the unseasonably warm spring day. Fishing, laughing, skipping rocks. From where he was, Thomas M. Jones could see that they hadn't caught anything yet.

The older boy had longish blond hair and was wearing a KISS T-shirt and cutoff jeans. The other boy — smaller, slighter, but also blond — wore a Star Wars T-shirt, with his jeans rolled up so he wouldn't get them wet. Through the scope, Jones thought they looked to be related. Maybe brothers.

When he was around their age, in places not far from Errol, he'd fished, too. But he was always alone. There had been no brother to fish with. There should have been, but there wasn't. Remembering, his index finger moved on the trigger, just a little.

He had hauled in smallmouth bass, brook trout, brown trout, rainbow trout — a few times, even landlocked salmon — and felt the rush of victory, the triumph that follows the long wait. But there had been no one to show the catch to. His father was almost always away, bartering for eggs or lamp oil or whatever. And his mother was always in the little shack — no running water, no electricity — recovering from whatever had been her latest setback. She was weak.

Thomas M. Jones would trek back through the woods, his catch flopping around in the bottom of a plastic bucket. His mother would see him and smile and beckon, asking to see what he'd caught. He'd place the bucket at her feet, wordless, and then stalk back into the woods.

He could always feel her hurt eyes on his back. And, as he stepped out of the clearing where they camped out, and into the woods again, he wondered if she was crying. Again.

He had hoped so.

The boys, Jones noted, weren't very good at fishing. They talked too much, too loudly — and skipping rocks across the water's surface probably didn't help, either. He placed the scope's crosshairs over the head of the younger boy, who looked intensely happy, totally indifferent to whether they caught any trout or not. Thomas M. Jones disliked that. What was the purpose of hunting or fishing if not to triumph over some wild thing? He was mystified by that attitude. It irritated him.

He moved into a shooting stance. Still within the shadows of the trees but with a better view of his target, he controlled his breathing and brought the Winchester up.

He did not miss.

CHAPTER 24

By the time he stepped out of the woods — hands up, a copy of his finished manuscript in one hand, a copy of *The Patriot Diaries* in the other — Thomas M. Jones looked ready.

We watched it unfold on TV. The whole fucking world watched it on TV. It was his big coming-out party.

An army of FBI agents and state and local cops were there to greet Thomas M. Jones, with guns drawn. The authorities hadn't told any media about their big event, but a Portland CBS reporter had heard something on the police scanner and had hustled up the Maine turnpike toward Errol, New Hampshire, following the armada of cop cars. His live feed was picked up by every network in the U.S., Canada, and Europe, the words "EXCLUSIVE CBS LIVE REPORT" crawling across the bottom of the screen. We were all in the Upchucks' basement, watching it on their old console TV.

The CBS guy hadn't been allowed to get too close, but he was close enough that we could see Thomas M. Jones. "He looks triumphant," I said, repulsed.

"He is," X said, arms crossed. Everyone was there: Patti, Sister Betty, Sam, Luke, Mike the Biker, and me and Jess. "This is his big day."

In fact, Jones looked like he didn't have a care in the world. One of the cops was shouting and gesturing at him. So, Thomas M. Jones stopped moving forward, his arms still up, the two books still held overhead. He was wearing cargo shorts, well-worn hiking boots, and a T-shirt. The trucker hat Jones wore had an upside-down peace symbol on it. That, X told me, was the logo of the National Alliance. Bob Cox's wife had told X that Jones had been wearing that same hat the morning of the bombing. It was the leader of the National Alliance who had written *The Patriot Diaries*.

We figure Cox had told the FBI about the symbol, too, and that Laverty would have figured out the connection right away. But only X had been able to figure out Jones's true identity. He told us all how he and the guys had convinced Tim Reid, the Klan member-slash-informant, to give up the list of names of the men who had ordered copies of the book.

Looking pleased with himself, Mr. Reid had been extracting his room key from his pocket after the feds had left when he looked up to see X holding up a reporter's notepad on which he had written, in black marker, the unlisted phone number of the Grand Wizard of the United Klans of America. "Give me what you gave Savoie and Laverty," X told him, "or my friends and I are going to phone your boss in Alabama and tell him you're a police informant."

X had then pointed across the Holiday Inn parking lot to where Sam Shiller and Luke Macdonald were standing by a pay phone, waving. Sam was holding a Polaroid camera and Luke was holding up some Polaroid snapshots — presumably of Tim Reid with an FBI special agent and a Portland police detective.

Reid promptly gave X what he wanted.

Reid's list had contained the name, or alias, of every guy who had purchased *The Diaries* from the United Klans of America in Mobile, Alabama. For New Hampshire and Maine, there had been only two dozen names, give or take, along with addresses and phone numbers.

Beside some of the phone numbers, someone had written letters and initials in faint pencil. Beside the name Thomas M. Jones had used, Reid had written "NA." The cops had probably thought it meant "no answer." X knew it meant "National Alliance."

And that's how X had learned the bomber's real name.

But as I later read in the Portland rags, Detective Savoie, to be fair, was the first one to spot Jones on video from the trucks-only lane at the Kittery toll booth. And then there were the two brothers who had been fishing in the Androscoggin. They told the cops where Thomas M. Jones was camping out. Apparently, that information earned them a ton of reward money.

Thomas M. Jones was an expert shot, and he hit his target. Using the scope on the Winchester Model 70, Jones had fired a single round at exactly the spot in the river where the Marquis lay submerged.

KEE-RANG.

The magnum round found its mark. It struck the big wraparound driver-side tail light sticking out of the water and shattered it to pieces. Some of the red plastic floated up to the surface of the Androscoggin River and started to float away.

The shot rang out like thunder, echoing for a couple of seconds. The youngest boy called out to his brother, terrified. They'd heard gunshots before. The older boy didn't hesitate. He rushed to his little brother, put an arm around him, and then pulled him down behind a fallen tree. He said Jones then stood up and waved at them, smiling. "Sorry to scare you boys. Run home and tell your parents that you just saw Thomas M. Jones."

The boys left behind their fishing rods and tackle box and ran like hell back home to tell their parents about the man in the woods. And their parents had immediately called the police.

So, that's how it went down. X knew his name, Savoie knew his face, but it was the two little boys who knew where to find him. It wasn't long before about a hundred cops and FBI agents descended on the spot where Thomas M. Jones was waiting for them.

When the first officers showed up, they said Jones was calmly sitting against a tree at the edge of the woods reading *The Patriot Diaries.*

CHAPTER 25

The courthouse occupied almost an entire city block in downtown Portland, rising above Federal and Newbury Streets like a monolith. It was here that Thomas M. Jones would spend most of the next few months of his life, and where the attention of all of the United States — and much of the world — would be focused.

The three-story building that housed the court was constructed of cold grey stone and had barred windows. On one side was Lincoln Park and on the other, an obstructed view of Casco Bay. On the Federal Street side, a string of Doric-style columns stretched up to the sky. The columns were capped with plain-looking capitals, the big circular stones that were supposed to hold up the upper expanse of the courthouse. The building looked like it was designed by a military commander to be a fort or something. It radiated formality and coldness, which I suppose was the idea.

Courtroom one was in a state of total chaos. People shouted, elbows were raised, curses were heard. Security was mediating disputes and, when necessary, ejecting those who were behaving badly. The cause of the chaos was easy to see: there were way more people in attendance than there were available seats. There was room to accommodate just shy of two hundred people, but ten times that number wanted to get in and see history being made.

Dozens of journalists were there, and they weren't going to miss a single moment; all of the national networks had dispatched their marquee reporters to cover the first court appearance of Thomas M. Jones, the accused Portland bomber.

Every Portland lawyer and court clerk who could be there was there, too, and they had lined up before dawn for the best seats. Some of the local railbirds — mainly retired folks who whiled away the hours watching criminal trials — had even gotten there before the lawyers and clerks. Security was frantically trying to set up an overflow room in courtroom eight on the second floor. They'd rigged up an audio link to courtroom one, but nobody wanted to listen to the proceedings. They wanted to see what was happening.

X, Jessie, and Leah were there with me — X to write about Thomas M. Jones's first court appearance, and me and Jessie and Leah just to see what the bastard looked like close up. Sam, Luke, and the Upchucks had all said they wouldn't come. "I'm worried I'll jump over the railing and kill the fucker with my bare hands," Patti had said, looking like she meant it. Sister Betty agreed.

We loitered in the hallway just outside the courtroom, watching the security staff search people's bags and wave metal-detector wands over them. I eyed the doors to the courtroom, which were being held open by the bodies moving in and out. Lawyers, clerks, and members of the media jostled for seats, growling at each other.

"If any of us get in, it should be you, X," I said. "You're here to write about it. The rest of us can sit in the overflow room upstairs." Leah and Jessie nodded.

As we stood there, figuring out what to do, Chief Chow marched in, two uniformed Portland cops on his heels. He saw us right away and walked over. "X, Mr. Blank," he said, extending his hand. "How are you?"

"Fine," X said, and introduced Jessie and Leah. "Is this bail hearing going to happen?"

Chow smiled. "It has to," he said. "The accused has been in custody for a day. The Eighth Amendment requires a bail hearing, even for him."

X had his notepad out and was scribbling away. The rest of us kept quiet, watching the exchange. "He can be considered for bail, even in a case of a mass murder?" X asked.

"This is a Harnish bail proceeding," Chow explained. "Murder used to be a capital offense in the state of Maine. A Harnish hearing determines whether the accused is facing what used to be a capital offense. If he is, then there's no right to bail."

"Chief, he killed over a hundred people. Isn't this all a waste of time?" I asked.

Chow smiled. "No comment, Kurt. Now, excuse me, I need to speak with DA Martin."

As Chow and his police escorts headed toward the stairs, none of the network reporters followed. I don't think they even recognized the chief. *What a bunch of goofs*, I thought.

The District Attorney's offices were directly across the hall from courtroom one. Savoie and Laverty were inside waiting for DA Sharon Martin.

When she finally stalked into her office, the DA said a curt hello and took a seat behind the large desk. She sighed as she flipped open a thick folder containing the grand jury's indictment of the young man who called himself Thomas M. Jones. "Well, the defense is going to try to turn this into a media circus," she said.

"It already is," Laverty pointed out. "That's unavoidable."

Savoie, looking like he had slept in his Oldsmobile, sounded unconcerned. "I don't think we need to worry about the media, ma'am. We've got this guy dead to rights. He did it. He even brags about it in his so-called manifesto."

"Yes, Detective," Martin said. "But we only have a single witness, this Mr. Cox, who sustained a serious knock on the head and hasn't been a hundred percent certain in his identification of the perpetrator. Granted, we've also got the motel and truck rental clerks, but I don't feel either of them is a very strong witness. Plus we've got some circumstantial evidence, but it's not exactly cut and dry."

"But we've got his autobiography," Savoie said. "He admits it all in there. End of story, I'd say."

"Not quite," Martin said, tapping another document on her desk. This one wasn't as imposing as the indictment, but it was thick enough. "We got served with this last night."

"What is it?" Laverty asked.

"A motion to exclude the manuscript," Martin said, handing the document across. "It's brilliant, actually."

Laverty scanned the first page and frowned. "Privileged? How can anyone argue the manuscript is privileged? He was holding it when we arrested him."

The DA sighed and shook her head. "Because Jones wrote it in the form of a long letter to his attorney, and for that reason they say it's protected by attorney-client privilege."

"And I see his attorney is none other than David Dennison. Interesting ..."

Laverty had had several run-ins with lawyer David Dennison over the years, and she did not like him one bit.

Dennison and Partners was a notorious New York City criminal defense firm that Dennison owned and operated. The firm actually had no partners — Dennison refused to give up any equity to anyone — but it was wildly successful. What the other associates lacked in equity was more than made up for in salary. The top tier associates at Dennison and Partners were paid better than most partners at every other New York criminal defense firm. Dennison could afford it.

With his chiseled jaw, six-pack abs, and Hollywood good looks, Dennison had been a high school football star. He had done his undergrad at Yale, studied law at Harvard, and clerked for a Supreme Court justice. On paper, and probably in real life, David Dennison could have been a candidate for the presidency, or a billionaire, or the CEO of a flourishing Fortune 500 company. But from his earliest days, it seems Dennison was drawn to something far more mundane: press clippings. He was always in the paper, saying provocative things about monstrous clients, making appearances on the evening news, extolling yet another legal victory, and racking up win after win. More than money, more than power, more than the beautiful call girls he reportedly summoned to his Fifth Avenue penthouse, David Dennison seemed to be drawn to fame like a fly to horseshit.

Fame or infamy, Laverty didn't think it made any difference to Dennison, as long as he was being talked about, watched, and reported on. He seemed better at being famous than being a criminal defense lawyer, though he was still a very good lawyer. For the most part, he appeared to have no ideology, no passion for one partisan cause or another. He had no core beliefs about anything, really, except one, Laverty thought as she flipped through his firm's client lists. She'd already noticed that every lawyer who worked at Dennison and Partners was male. And it was clear to her that every client Dennison had represented was male. So, she suspected that there was one view that David Dennison shared with his newest client, Thomas M. Jones: that women were inferior to men.

CHAPTER 26

We sat at the back of courtroom one — me, X, Jessie, and Leah. We'd slipped in just as they were closing the doors. X had his pen and notepad out, so we kind of looked like we might be media. Nobody paid any attention to us anyway.

When Thomas M. Jones was first brought in, there was an audible intake of breath from some in the assembled crowd. But after he was led to the prisoner's box and seated, other than some rustling of papers and a bit of murmuring, the crowd remained quiet, like they were in church or something.

This was the first time anyone outside of law enforcement had seen Thomas M. Jones up close in person. He appeared unremarkable. He was shackled, hands and feet, and was wearing an orange jumpsuit. Four security officers surrounded him, partially blocking our view.

But when the lawyer hustled over to confer with his client, the two guards at the front stepped back and we could see Jones better. He stared straight ahead as his lawyer whispered in his ear. He didn't nod or respond in any way.

The judge's chair was empty; he hadn't arrived yet. But in the cordoned-off area at the front, two clerks had positioned themselves below the flags of the United States and the state of Maine. The defense team and the prosecution sat patiently waiting.

One of the clerks, an older, pudgy guy with a handlebar moustache, approached the rail that divided the room. "Judge O'Sullivan will be here shortly," he announced. "This is a reminder that talking, smoking, and chewing gum are not permitted in the court. And everyone must rise when the judge enters."

At that, I looked over at Jessie and laughed. I couldn't help myself. Jessie was chewing gum. If she wasn't smoking, Jessie was always chewing gum.

When we turned back to the courtroom, we saw that Thomas M. Jones had swiveled his head around and was now staring directly at us. Everyone else in the courtroom turned to see what Jones was looking at.

Jessie and I had debated whether she should even come. If he was the one who had raped her on the side of a road so long ago, I told her, being there might be too upsetting. But Jessie, who was mostly fearless, had been adamant. "This fucker doesn't control me," she said. "He did for a few minutes, one night, but not for one second since. If it's him, I want to go and show him he doesn't scare me." So here she was, with me and X and Leah beside her.

The long silence of the courtroom was broken by the voice of Thomas M. Jones, reedy and still youthful. "Jessie?" he said, loud enough for everyone to hear.

X and I looked at each other.

Holy shit.

The media reacted immediately, though thankfully they couldn't exactly rush over to find out who Jessie was. But within seconds, Laverty and Savoie hurried over to us. "Excuse me, Miss," Laverty said quietly, ignoring the rest of us. She wasn't a big fan of the X Gang, you might say. "Was the accused addressing you just now?"

"Who are you?" Jessie asked.

"Sorry. Special Agent Theresa Laverty, FBI. This is Detective Savoie. Can you tell us why the accused addressed you? How do you know him?"

Jessie looked over at me. I cleared my throat. "It might be better if we talk somewhere more private," I said, then pointed at Savoie. "But not him — just you, me, and Jessie."

"Fine," Laverty said. She led me and Jessie out of the courtroom and through the crowd of people still milling about outside. A couple of reporters ran out after us barking questions at Jessie, but Laverty ushered us through a set of double doors marked *No Entry* and into what looked like a combination library and boardroom. She closed the door behind us, extended her hand to Jessie, and introduced herself formally.

She then waved us toward a couple of empty chairs. "And you are?"

"Jessie ... Jessie Jett."

"Jett?" Laverty said, arching an eyebrow.

"Jett," Jessie said, deadpan.

"O-kay," Laverty said, clearly unconvinced. "Why did Jones just say your name, Jessie?"

Jessie looked at me, uncertain. I nodded. Laverty, I figured, could be trusted, sort of.

"I know him, or at least I used to know him."

"How did you know him?"

"When I was in high school, I lived in Clinton, in Kennebec County," Jessie said. "I worked in the library there, after school."

"Jones lived there, too?"

"Near there," Jessie said. "In the woods."

"With his family?"

"Yeah," Jessie said. "They squatted in a shack in the woods, basically. But I'd see him at the library after school."

"Did he go to your school?"

"I never saw him there," Jessie said. "I think his parents home-schooled him."

"Why would he go to the library?" Laverty asked.

"He was smart. He knew a lot."

"Like what?"

"Like everything," Jessie said. "He read a ton of books — Shakespeare, poetry, classical stuff, all of that. He read because he wanted to, he said, not because he had to."

Laverty hesitated before asking, "Was he your friend? Your ... boyfriend?"

Jessie laughed out loud at that. I smiled. "I'm not into boys so much, Agent Laverty," she said. "Not my thing."

At that point, Laverty visibly relaxed and smiled.

"It's cool," I said to Jessie, nodding in Laverty's direction. "Not an issue with Agent Laverty."

The two women exchanged a look, and Jessie continued, "So, no, he wasn't a boyfriend or anything. He was just a friend, back then."

Laverty nodded. "Did he have any unusual ... ideas ... back then? Was he involved in any political groups that you know of?"

"He wasn't involved in anything that I knew of," Jessie said. "But he did have lots of weird ideas. That was okay, at first. But later on it started to make me uncomfortable."

"Racism, anti-Semitism? Stuff like that?"

"Yeah," Jessie said. "At the end, lots of that shit. He changed."

"How?"

Jessie frowned, remembering. "He got ... *angrier*," she said. "It was like he found a religion or something."

"Can you give me an example?"

"Immigrants, refugees, Jews, gay people, all of that," she said. "He started to rail against them a lot when we talked. But there was one group he hated the most ..." She hesitated.

"Who?"

Jessie looked upset for the first time. "Women," she said, finally. "Females. Girls. He started getting really critical of women in general."

"Why?" Laverty asked, then she abruptly changed course. Sensing something, she leaned forward a bit. "Jessie, did something happen?"

Jessie looked down at the floor. I put a hand on her arm. "Yes," she said.

"Did he hurt you?"

"Yes."

"Did he —" Laverty started to say.

Jessie cut her off. "Yes. Yes, yes, yes!" she said, eyes blazing. "The bastard raped me!"

Laverty looked shocked but also like she wanted to hug her. "I'm so sorry, Jessie," she said. "I'm sorry to have to ask you these questions ..."

"It's okay," Jessie said. After a long pause, she took a deep breath and continued. "He raped me after work one night. He pulled me into the woods and did it." She looked at me, and her face was sad. "He was strong. I couldn't fight him."

I reached over and hugged her. "It's not your fault, Jess."

"I know it isn't!" Jess snapped, pulling away.

Laverty nodded. "Kurt, I think it would be better if I conduct a formal interview with Jessie — in private."

I looked at Jessie. "You cool with that?"

She nodded.

Theresa Laverty stood up. "I need to get back in the courtroom to speak with some of my colleagues," she said. "Can we reconnect in a day or two?"

"Sure," Jessie said.

Laverty pointed in the direction of courtroom one. "The media will probably swarm you if you go back in there," she said. "And I think you will need to stay away if we decide to proceed with charges."

"Charges?"

"New charges, for assaulting you," Laverty said, her jaw set. "There's no statute of limitations on rape, Jessie. And the prosecution might be able to use this to their advantage."

CHAPTER 27

Laverty looked at the monitor showing Thomas M. Jones sitting on the bunk in the fortified cell, ramrod straight, hands folded in his lap. He was wearing an oversized orange jumpsuit and flip flops that were too big. He sat staring at the wall, unmoving.

She was told he hadn't eaten for a day.

Laverty and Savoie were in a tiny room just down the hall from the holding cell at the Cumberland County courthouse. Two security officers stood by the door.

"He just sits there like he's in a trance or something," one officer told them. "Like a goddamn statue. He's refusing food."

Laverty kept watching Jones on the grainy black-and-white screen. "So, he says he won't eat until he gets some books?"

"Not just any books," the officer said. "He has a list. Says his lawyer has it."

"What's on it?" Laverty asked.

"Classical stuff. Old stuff," the officer said, sounding unimpressed.

Laverty glanced over at the burly courthouse officer. She couldn't picture him reading any book, let alone an old classical one.

Laverty turned back to the monitor and studied the younger man closely. After it had taken so long to find him, it was hard to believe he was finally there in front of her.

Jones stood just under six feet tall and was in impressive shape — lean, tanned, and muscled, but not too muscular. He looked like someone who lived entirely outdoors and ate only healthy foods. Reddish-brown hair was close-cropped above his narrow face. His nose was aquiline, almost delicate, but he had a strong jawline, which was presently unshaven.

Jones's eyes were pale blue, and Laverty found them off-putting. He hadn't spoken since being taken into custody, except to ask for his lawyer and the books; he'd just sat there silently, staring unblinking at his interrogators.

He had no tattoos, but they had noticed a small symbol on his right forearm, about an inch in length. It had been mistaken for a scar, at first. The symbol was a square, with what appeared to be two feet in one corner.

"What is that?" Savoie had asked after a uniformed cop gave them a Polaroid.

"It's the Elder Futhark Odal rune," Laverty told him.

"What the fuck is … the elder what?"

"They call it the Othala rune," she said, squinting at the photo. "It's a Viking symbol, third century. The

Waffen SS used it on their uniforms and insignia. Nazi death squads appropriated it during the war and wore it in Croatia and places like that. Neo-Nazis use it here in the States, in South Africa, in Germany."

"What's it mean?"

"Homeland," she said. "Their inherited white homeland."

Savoie stared at the photo. "It's not a tattoo?" he asked.

"No," Laverty said. "It's been carved into his skin."

CHAPTER 28

Jessie joining the Hot Nasties wasn't all that difficult. It just sort of happened. But Your Humble Narrator re-joining the band? That, as it turned out, was a lot more difficult.

I had been invited to become a Hot Nasty after Jimmy Cleary was killed. He was my friend, and he'd been their lead singer. I'd been in another sort-of-seminal Portland punk band, the Social Blemishes, who weren't anything like the Nasties. The Nasties were the local punk Beatles, more or less, and the Blemishes were the Stooges before they got a record contract. The Nasties were tight and disciplined and had great tunes. The Social Blemishes were raw and raucous and we sounded like a Mack truck full of squealing pigs slamming into a glass factory at two hundred miles an hour.

But I knew all the Nasties' songs. I knew all the lyrics. And — with Stiff Records offering to sign them to a two-record deal, and maybe more — I knew I could help them out.

It worked out at first. We were pretty much punk rock gods for a while. Had an actual professional-type tour around New England and parts of Canada. Played big shows with some big bands, like the Teen Idles, who would go on to become the hottest hardcore band of the moment, Minor Threat. We got to stay in real hotels (sort of). We had a real tour manager (sort of). We started to generate real buzz (sort of).

But then everything went to total rat shit. It fell apart. We weren't as slick as the new wave bands, and we weren't as raw as the hardcore bands. We were stuck in the middle, not belonging to either genre and therefore no longer cool. We were the punk rock meat in the new wave/hardcore sandwich. Stiff dropped us because we were over before we'd even gotten a chance to be the next new thing.

The rest of the guys were super bummed out, to be sure. Sam and Luke had to get real jobs, doing inventory at the Sears at the Maine Mall. Eddie started working construction for his dad and spent all of his free time with his new girlfriend, Nagamo.

And me? Well, you know where I ended up. Go big or go home, I always say.

The first time I ever got really fucked up, it was doing speed. You don't really get addicted to speed — you just develop a dependency on it. As luck might have it, I became *really, really* dependent on it. I ended up OD'ing and wound up in the hospital in Toronto during the tour.

My friends and bandmates hauled me out of the hospital, where I'd been manacled to a bed, and dragged my shriveled carcass to the Six Nations of Grand River. It was there, about ninety minutes outside Toronto, where I went through this sweat lodge healing ceremony. And I actually got healed. For a while.

The Hot Nasties didn't kick me out that time.

But this time, after I disappeared on them and developed a fondness for the hardest hard drug, well, they gave up on me. Understandably, they moved on, figuring the Hot Nasties were dead. They figured I was dead, too — or soon would be.

But then I came back like a punk rock Lazarus.

So, what to do about Kurt Blank?

There were apparently many discussions about that, down in the dungeon at Sound Swap; much debate, much deliberation. Sam was fed up with me, Luke wanted me back. The Upchuck sisters, when asked for their opinions, insisted I deserved a second chance. X, meanwhile, would say nothing. When asked for his opinion, he refused. That was interpreted as a "no" vote.

So, I was summoned to the band summit. Jessie, too. She, as noted, was in.

Jessie was this kick-ass drummer, you see. She was a powerhouse. No fancy frills and rolls and shit. Just a straight-ahead beat machine. She drummed like heavy artillery. She drummed like a screen door in a hurricane. She drummed like a drum machine on meth.

"I can't believe a chick can drum so hard," Luke said to her the first time they all jammed together.

"I can't believe you play bass like a little girl," Jessie

said, deadpan. Sam and the Upchucks and I all burst out laughing. X even smiled at that one.

When Jessie and I arrived for the summit, everyone else was there already. Nobody said much. Sam and Luke were fiddling with their guitars, tuning up, while the Upchucks sat on the dirty old couch beside Mike the bouncer. X was sitting on the steps leading to the shared practice space, and Leah was on the stair below him, leaning against the brick wall.

Jessie squeezed past X and Leah and headed to the battered drum kit. She started fiddling with the tuning of the floor tom.

"So," I finally said, "I guess I'm here to apply for a job I previously held."

Nobody laughed. Sister Betty looked up at me. "Are you ready, babe?" She only called me "babe" when she was worried about me. She'd been calling me babe a lot in recent months.

"I think so," I said. "I feel okay."

Sister Betty looked at me intently. She, I figured, had volunteered to be my inquisitor. I was okay with that. Better her than X.

"Kurt, we all love you, you know that, right?"

Here it comes, I thought. "I know," I said. "I love you guys, too." Pause. "Even Luke."

Sam and Mike laughed at that one, but Sister Betty didn't. She plunged forward. "What you did after Stiff dropped the Nasties, babe?" she said. "What you did to yourself? It was totally unacceptable."

"Totally fucking unacceptable," Sam said. Luke nodded.

"Life throws all kinds of shit at you," she said. "People break up. People are mean. Record labels drop bands." She was looking pretty angry at this point. She pointed a finger at me. "None of that justifies taking off on your friends and becoming a fucking heroin addict, Kurt." There was a long silence. No one moved a muscle, and definitely not me.

Sister Betty glared at me, her painted black fingernail still pointing at me. "Nothing justifies that!" she said, her voice shaking. "Nothing!"

At Casco Bay, ironically enough, we had been prepped for this sort of thing. You know, the highly uncomfortable encounter with upset family and friends. "You have hurt them!" Drill Sergeant Paula had hollered at us. "You have let them down! Be prepared for them to be angry with you for a long time! Maybe forever! They are justified! They are entitled!"

Sister Betty was angry. So were the rest of them. I could feel it. Their anger, in fact, was like the heat from the crowd at a packed show, flashing up between songs.

I hesitated. I'd been expecting this moment, and preparing for it, but it was still hard to hear.

"Guys," I croaked, "I love this band. I love playing. I love all of it." Pause. "When Stiff dropped us, it felt like the world had ended —"

"Kurt, that is such bullshit!" Sister Betty yelled, cutting me off. I'd never seen her this pissed off before. She pointed around the room at the assembled Hot Nasties and Punk Rock Virgins and assorted others. "We are each other's world! Us! Not some fucking record label!"

She was right, of course.

I tried again. "I know. I get it. It's just that if I play again, I'm afraid I'll get back into bad habits again." I could see that some of them were surprised by that. They had been expecting me to beg to be let back in. But it was the opposite. I kept going. "I want to play with you guys again. But I'm not sure I should." At that, X turned and looked straight at me for the first time. He fixed those unblinking, uneven pupils on me, the ones that still made me feel as uncomfortable as they did back in grade seven. "That's the only thing you could say," he said, "that suggests you might actually be ready … the realization that you may never be. That this," X waved at Sam, Luke, and Jessie, "isn't right for you anymore."

"Maybe it isn't," I said after a long pause. "I want to come back, but I don't want to get fucked up again."

Anyway, I went for a walk. They took a vote.

I was back in if I wanted to be.

CHAPTER 29

"An important part of the rehabilitation process is for inmates to keep their personal friendships and relationships healthy through communication," Laverty read in the Inmate Mail Policy of the Maine Department of Corrections. "All inmates are allowed to send and receive mail from anyone, with the exception of correspondence between an inmate and another inmate, an inmate and their victim, and/or a person who is prohibited contact by court order. If an inmate does not have any money in their commissary account for postage, they will be allowed to send two free letters per week."

Laverty sighed. Almost from the moment he had arrived at the bunker deep in the bowels of the Cumberland County courthouse, Thomas M. Jones had been receiving mail. And lots of it. A loose-lipped corrections worker had informed her that he'd received letters from people who wanted to kill him and from people who wanted to understand him — from students writing their criminology master's thesis to reporters seeking exclusive interviews. He'd even gotten a couple of offers of marriage.

This created a problem, she thought, and meetings were convened with serious-sounding people with seriously important titles. Should the man accused of the worst mass murder in the recent history of the United States of America be permitted to receive mail? Should he be allowed to send letters, particularly when he was standing trial for slaughtering 121 innocent people?

But the mail policy was clear: all inmates were allowed to send and receive mail. *All of them.* Even the ones who had no interest in "keeping personal friendships" or maintaining "healthy relationships." (Thomas M. Jones didn't have any of those, Laverty figured.)

After his mini-hunger-strike, Jones had gotten access to some of the books he had requested. He was also given access to old newspapers and magazines (though all of the articles about the bombing had been removed). But it was the letters, Laverty was informed, that Thomas M. Jones enjoyed reading the most. He'd even started to answer some of them.

All of his mail was opened, inspected, and read before he received it. Any mail that appeared to be written in some secret code or foreign language was treated as contraband and was kept by the Department of Corrections. So, too, were the letters that suggested other people whom Thomas M. Jones could murder when he got out. But most of the letters — even the ones that praised him — got through. Jones still had rights, after all.

The cell Jones was being kept in was located on the basement level of the courthouse and had been designed for solitary confinement. It was thought he was more likely to survive there than at the Cumberland County Jail or the Maine State Prison. There had apparently been many inmates threatening to kill him if they got the chance.

Soon after his hearing, Laverty was allowed down there again, and when she peered through the smudged, shatterproof observation window, she saw Thomas M. Jones sitting on a metal stool reading his letters, a stack of correspondence neatly piled beside him.

CHAPTER 30

In 1981, people cared about popular movies (like *Raiders of the Lost Ark*). They cared about the price of gas ($1.25 a gallon). They cared about the stupid faraway wedding of Charles and Diana, for fuck sakes. They cared about the space shuttle (the first one, *Columbia*). They cared about the possibly imminent collapse of communism (in Poland). They cared about some lunatic shooting the Pope (he survived). And they cared, of course, about the murder of more than one hundred men, women, and children at the Portland YWCA. That's what they cared about.

I cared, too, of course, because two of my friends had died. But I also cared about Jessie, who'd been a different kind of victim. The girls in the Punk Rock Virgins all cared, too — Patti Upchuck in particular — that Jessie had been raped. The Nasties all cared, of course, because Jessie was one of them now, and Sam and Luke wanted to protect her — even though she didn't need protection. And X cared in his own way, having always had zero tolerance for those who use violence against women and girls.

But the outside world? They didn't seem to give a shit. The *Portland Daily Sun*, which was a nasty little right-wing tabloid, called Thomas M. Jones's outburst in court "a distraction" and "a possible defense tactic." The morons who made up the *Daily Sun*'s editorial board wanted the murder trial to proceed, and the "long-ago alleged rape" put on the legal back burner. Or dropped entirely.

Anonymous sources in the other Portland paper, the *Press Herald*, were similarly indifferent. Nameless defense attorneys suggested that it was all a stunt cooked up by Jones's high-paid New York City lawyer, David Dennison. "It's a transparent tactic to divert everyone's attention from the main act," sniffed one anonymous attorney. "It means that Dennison doesn't have much of a defense."

In the spectators' benches in courtroom one, no one else seemed to give a shit, either. They were there for a murder trial, and they wanted the murder trial to get underway, right away. The rape of a girl with a drinking problem who dresses like a boy? *Who cares*, they probably thought.

Out on Portland's streets, almost everyone felt the same way. They wanted to see Thomas M. Jones hanging from the bell tower at the Cathedral of the Immaculate Conception. In 1981, as the guys in the X Gang soon discovered, sexual assault wasn't seen as that big a deal by most people.

Bizarrely, there was one person who seemed a bit indifferent to it all. And it shocked the hell out of me and the guys in the X Gang, to tell you the truth: Jessie.

I'd been right beside her in court when Jones saw her and called out her name. I'd been with her, too, when Laverty grilled her — and, later, I was loitering nearby when she was interviewed by the DA and two of her assistants. And when she was chased along the street by a gaggle of reporters asking who she was and what she knew about the Portland bomber. I had been with her for just about every moment since we got out of Casco Bay, in fact. I'd been with Jessie through all of that, and she didn't once break a sweat, other than that one time when we were talking to Laverty. She'd been raped by one of the worst mass murderers in U.S. history, and she didn't seem to me to be the least bit upset about it. She just always seemed to be totally in control.

I thought this was a bit weird, actually, so I spoke to Patti about it, because I knew Patti could relate. We were at Sound Swap, and the rest of the gang was out getting something to eat at Michael's up the street. The two of us were sitting surrounded by stacks of used LPs on the main floor. The lights were off, and the place was totally quiet.

"I'm confused by something," I said. "Jessie —"

Patti finished my sentence for me. "Jessie isn't reacting to what happened like you expect her to?"

I looked at her, surprised. "How'd you know?"

"Guys expect girls who've been assaulted to be vulnerable, so they can protect them and all that," she said, smiling. "Even gay guys."

"Well, I'm sorry for being predictable and all that, but I *do* want to protect her." I was feeling a bit defensive. "I mean, have you seen the shit they've been printing in the *Sun* and the *Press Herald* about it?"

Patti shook her head. "No. I couldn't care less what a bunch of old farts think about what should happen," she said. "Men are always telling women what should happen to women — especially when it comes to our bodies and sex. Fuck them."

"But what about Jessie?" I said, exasperated. "I know for a fact that the ..." I stammered, because I didn't even want to say the word. "What happened to her had a major impact on her. It definitely played a role in her turning to booze and all that."

"I don't doubt it."

"So, why isn't she more upset? Why doesn't she want to kill that bastard with her bare hands, like we do, like I would if I got half a chance? I just don't get it," I said. "She's so calm."

Patti put a hand on my arm. "Kurt, babe, Jessie's just coping. She's totally fucking brave. I can honestly tell you that if I ever saw those two bastards who raped me again, I'd probably fall apart. I'd be a mess." She paused. "For Jessie to be able to keep her cool through all of this — with the cops asking questions, the trial — it's totally amazing. It shows how strong she is."

"Well, I'm worried about her falling off the wagon again," I said. "The pressure has to be intense."

We could hear the rest of the Nasties and the Virgins returning from Michael's. Patti stood up. "The rest of us are worried about you, too, my friend," she said, her voice low. "We don't have anything to worry about, do we?"

"No, no," I said, feeling a flash of irritation. "I'm sober as a fucking judge. I'm more straight edge than X. I'm just worried about Jess."

"All of us are. We're her friends now, too."

Everyone came crashing through the door, laughing and chattering.

"We've got her back. And yours," she whispered to me.

CHAPTER 31

While Thomas M. Jones's outburst at his bail hearing had delayed the start of the trial — resulting in several angry phone calls to Martin from the mayor of Portland, the governor, and even the two senators representing the state of Maine — Martin and her two assistant DAs believed every word of Jessie's story. And the more they heard, the more convinced they became that the rape charge needed to be added to the 121 charges of felony murder and 311 counts of attempted murder that Thomas M. Jones was already facing. A meeting was called to inform Jones's lawyer, David Dennison, of their decision. It wasn't going well and voices were raised.

Dennison picked up a tattered copy of *The Maine Rules of Unified Criminal Procedure* and slammed it on the floor of the Cumberland County District Attorney's boardroom. The conversation stopped.

"I would thank you, Mr. Dennison, not to throw things in my boardroom," Martin said, her eyes and voice icy. "And I would also appreciate a more civil tone." She paused. "You are very lucky your client isn't also facing a charge of sexually abusing a minor."

"That's bullshit and you know it!" Dennison snapped, leaning forward in an effort to intimidate Martin. "The complainant was sixteen, the age of consent in this backward state, when she had consensual sex with my client! And —"

But the DA wasn't fazed and shot back. "She was not sixteen, Mr. Dennison! It was a week before her birthday. She was fifteen at the time," Martin hissed. "And it wasn't in any way consensual."

Dennison and Martin glared at each other. Their associates glared at each other, too. The trial hadn't even started, and both sides already deeply despised each other. After a moment, Dennison's associate, Mr. Popowich, reached down to retrieve the copy of *The Maine Rules of Unified Criminal Procedure.*

"This is prosecutorial overkill," Dennison said, eyes narrowing. "He's already facing dozens of murder and attempted murder charges. You can only hang him once, Miss Martin. What possible value does this rape charge have, other than to inflame the females in the jury pool?"

"So, your client doesn't intend to sign a jury trial waiver then, I take it?" Martin asked. "That was one of the questions we had for you today."

"We haven't decided yet," Dennison said, leaning back in the boardroom chair, feeling in charge again.

"But we have a grave concern about this stunt, Miss Martin, and the obvious attempt you are making to turn this trial into a war of the sexes." He paused. "That is a war you won't win. I assure you."

The DA resisted the temptation to roll her eyes. Dennison's preferred approach to trials was well known: pit men against women. Given the fact that men completely dominated the justice system, criminal and otherwise, it was an approach that had worked quite well so far.

"In comparative terms," Dennison sneered, "the alleged assault on Miss Jett — a lesbian, an alcoholic — is a waste of the court's time. It is an admission that your main case is weak, Miss Martin."

The DA was well aware that Dennison was trying to bait her into an outburst, but she bit her tongue. After spending hours with Jessie, Martin and her two associates knew that the rape could, indeed, be seen by the judge and a jury as a distraction. But they had become convinced it could be seen as something else, too. Something critically important: motive.

CHAPTER 32

I stood there, guitar in one hand, gear bag in the other, looking around.

Gary's. Home sweet punk home.

Everything at Gary's was both old and familiar. It was comforting, like an old pair of Converse. To my post-junkie eyes, though, it seemed a bit different now, and unsettling.

I was happy to be back there with my friends, naturally, getting ready to play the songs we'd written about the lives we knew — about relationships, about favorite *Star Trek* episodes, about how stupid grown-ups were, about going to the 7-Eleven late at night to get a Coke Slurpee and a bag of Cheetos. All that.

But being back there was more than a bit depressing, too. Everything we'd lost came back in rush: Jimmy Cleary, dead in the alleyway out back; Marky Upton, now gone, too, holding the door for me and X when we rushed out to find Jimmy; Danny O'Heran, playing at Gary's with me and the rest of the Social Blemishes before he got sick; and Eddie Igglesden and Nagamo. All of them were there just a moment ago, but now they were all gone.

Gary's was exquisitely, royally filthy, with dust and dirt everywhere. The carpet was so ancient, it was impossible to determine what color it had once been. The walls were the same, with yellowish stains and dark splotches of dried-up beer and whisky — and here and there, smears of what might have been either ketchup or dried blood.

The tables were tiny and round, barely big enough to hold an overflowing ashtray and a few empty glasses of draft, which got piled up in the middle. They'd been bolted to the floor — to prevent them from being used as battering rams in fights (which broke out frequently). The chairs were mismatched, ancient, and uncomfortable but not bolted down, so useful in a fight.

And the air? Well, the air was virtually unbreathable — a toxic, stultifying stew that was part cigarette smoke, part dust, and part sweat and piss. I closed my eyes and inhaled.

I loved it there.

I looked around, remembering when we first started hanging out there. At first, we'd been intimidated by the bikers — all of us, I guess, except X. (Gary's was originally a biker bar, but as their numbers had dwindled the owners had to make up the difference in revenue somehow.) Eventually, they became sort of amused by us and left us alone. Standing there, I remembered one early,

early Social Blemishes show where nobody was on the dance floor — except two hulking bikers in leather, and this balding, wiry little guy standing between them. The little guy was wearing a T-shirt with the letters "OFFO" across the front. The three of them just stood there, watching us get to the end of our set. And when we did, the little guy smiled, gave me a thumbs up, and the three of them ambled away.

Later, as we were carting our gear out to Eddie's van, Mike the bouncer approached me. "Do you know who that guy was who was watching you play?"

I shook my head.

"That was Tommy Blaine," he said. "The fucking boss."

"Of what?" I'd asked.

"The Outlaws," Mike said, rolling his eyes. "The 'OFFO' on his T-shirt means 'Outlaws Forever, Forever Outlaws.'"

"So? What's the big deal about him watching us?"

"You were in *his* house," Mike said, smiling through his big beard. "He was deciding whether he'd let you little freaks live or not." He paused, laughing. "You passed the test. You get to live a bit longer."

And freaks we were, I guess. In those days, in the early days of the Portland scene, the punks were this weird mix of Maine College of Art students, gays and lesbians, cross-dressers, poets, nonconformists, anarchists, socialists, the socially awkward, the alienated, the angry. But somehow we all got along.

And after Tommy Blaine decided to let us live, the bikers started to leave us alone, too. They'd stay up at the bar near the front doors, and we'd hang out around the stage and use the alleyway exit, taking care to avoid walking through their territory. Same with the bikers: they'd stay on their side, ignoring us.

Anyway, we got a place of our own, and the scene started to grow, and it took off like a teenage bottle rocket. *Boom.* What had been obscure and underground suddenly became cool and popular. And then — with new wave and hardcore hitting us from both sides — punk got obscure again.

I came back to the present. X had walked in and was standing looking at me.

"Hey," he said.

"Hey."

"You okay?"

"Yeah," I said. "Just remembering stuff."

He cocked an eyebrow, one of the main facial expressions in his repertoire. "Need help with your gear? I can't stay long."

I nodded. "Thanks. Yeah. It's good to be back."

CHAPTER 33

"NO NO NO NO NO! YOU PUNK!"

Now, this was going to be interesting.

"LISTEN, YOU LITTLE PUNK, YOU'RE GOING TO GET ARRESTED FOR INCITING A GOD-DAMNED RIOT, DO YOU UNDERSTAND ME? GET THESE PEOPLE OFF THIS STAGE NOW!"

I have to admit that the officer's bellowed threat sounded a lot more like an offer. To a rabble-rousing, currently stone-cold-sober punk rocker like me — and to the usually anti-social bunch of punks that made up the Hot Nasties — getting arrested for inciting a riot would have been pretty fucking cool.

I kept playing and kept hollering into the microphone center stage at Gary's, and kept looking at the cop, who in turn glowered back at me. He had his hand on his utility belt, which suggested to me that he was about to mace me, handcuff me, or shoot me. Any one of those things would have brought the Hot Nasties' big reunion show to a crashing halt, but — man! — what an amazing finish it would be! I kept playing. The cop kept glaring. The "rioters" kept "rioting."

It was a hot summer night in 1981, and the Nasties were onstage. The cheap bastards who owned Gary's had brought us back, I suppose, because they were interested in selling gallons of watered-down beer to the two hundred plus teenagers who had jammed into the place.

The Nasties didn't ask what their motivation was, frankly. For us, it was an opportunity to show off our new drummer, Jessie Jett. It was also a way to show everyone that the lead singer wasn't dead in a shooting gallery somewhere down in Florida. And, naturally, it was yet another way to spread discord and dissent — and maybe even start a riot — in the middle of the tourist-friendly destination that is the port area of Portland, Maine. A riot? Hell, we'd have paid to stir up shit on that scale.

But, still. Having the cops onstage with us probably made our point better than the scores of punks could. Our point being, punk *still* wasn't about being comfortable, or complacent, or entertained. It was about pissed-off young people shaking things up, and having a bit of fun, and maybe changing a few attitudes (and redressing a few injustices) along the way.

The cop stepped closer, menacingly, apparently intending to signal how serious he was about arresting me for inviting fans onto the stage to dance and thereby, to wit and henceforth, causing a "riot." I stopped playing and waved to the rest of the band to cease and desist. Our song, a locally popular three-chord screamer called "Invasion of the Tribbles," ground to an inglorious stop.

"Okay, okay," I said into the mic. I was wearing my favorite biker jacket, a Clash T-shirt, pink cowboy hat, and black jeans. The cop was big and towered above us, his back turned (rudely, I thought) to the couple hundred folks in attendance.

"I am going to be arrested for inciting a riot if you darn punks don't stop dancing and get off the stage." I paused and glanced at the cop, who seemed capable of murder at any moment. "You don't want me arrested, do you?" I asked the crowd.

A wild cheer went up.

"I thought so," I said. "But get off the fuckin' stage anyway, okay?"

The cops left without arresting anyone. But they hadn't really been there for us, for once.

They were there looking for another group of guys who took off the second they saw the police coming through Gary's main doors and shouldering their way through the sold-out crowd.

Here's what happened.

Historically, of course, we punks hated the cops, and the cops hated us. The only time Portland cops ever showed up at any of our shows was to crack heads — ours mostly. It had always been thus.

This show — the first Nasties gig in a long time, and with the ferocious and amazing Jessie Jett keeping the beat — was different.

The cops were there, you see, to keep us from getting *our* heads kicked in. Not to kick in our heads. As even X admitted, after the gig as we were packing up our gear, the Portland Police Department had probably prevented someone from getting hurt.

"It would've been bad," X said, helping us to carry amps and guitars out to the van we'd rented for the gig. "Really bad."

I had spotted them first, I think, because I was onstage and facing the crowd when they appeared. There were four of them. They'd slipped onto the dance floor and were standing up against the back wall. They were all wearing jean jackets and sweatshirts. They were white, youngish, muscular, and all had close-cropped hair. On cue — as we finished one song and before we could launch into another — they all took off their jackets and sweatshirts. And then they just stood there. They were all wearing black T-shirts. On the front of two of the T-shirts "NO MEANS YES" was written in big white letters. On the other two, "ANGRY WHITE MAN."

Angry white man was almost funny. It sounded like a skit on *Saturday Night Live* or something. But *no means yes* wasn't funny, not at all.

Patti Upchuck, who was standing on the side of Gary's stage, definitely didn't think so. She stepped up to Sam Shiller's mic before Sam even knew what was going on. "Hey, *motherfucker*!" she yelled, pointing at the guys. "No means no!"

One of the four guys, the stocky, short one, smirked. He put his hands around his mouth, to amplify what he was going to say, which was "Fuck you, you fucking dyke!"

"Fuck you, you fucking fuck!" Patti yelled back, livid.

Sister Betty was beside her now, along with a couple members of Tit Sweat. Jessie, meanwhile, was standing up at her drum kit, squinting in the direction of these four pieces of shit. "Get the fuck out of here!"

Patti started to move to the edge of the stage. The four guys looked amused. I grabbed her wrist and whispered in her ear. "Patti, don't! We don't know who the fuck these guys are. They could have knives or something. X isn't here. It's not worth it. Not for these assholes." I nodded in the direction of the crowd, most of whom were oblivious to what was going on up front. Mike the bouncer was quickly pushing his way through the throng, his lead-filled pool cue at his side. "Mike'll handle it ..."

Patti whirled on me, eyes flashing. "Kurt, let me go! I don't fucking need you or X to protect me." She pulled away and jumped off the stage. Sister Betty and the rest of the girls from the Virgins as well as Jessie weren't far behind. They were pissed off. I sighed and jumped off the stage, too.

But before they could get to the four idiots, Mike did. He got nose-to-nose with the short, stocky one. I couldn't hear what he said, but I could see the four of them simultaneously look down at Mike's pool cue.

They quickly conferred with each other, picked up their jackets and sweatshirts, and started moving toward the back door to a chorus of jeers and more than a few raised middle fingers.

Soon after they left, a couple of cops arrived and started pushing their way through the crowd, trying to get to the front of the stage. By the time they got to us — and by the time they got onto the stage, where I had invited a couple dozen punks to dance along to a celebratory rendition of "Invasion of the Tribbles" — the assholes were long gone.

But it wouldn't be the last time we'd see them.

Herewith, a confession.

The punk scene should have been misogyny-free. It should have been a safe haven from sexism. Punk should have been a movement where the genders, at long fucking last, were equal. But it wasn't.

I admit it: punk did not always live up to its promise. Punk was not everything I cracked it up to be. For women and girls, punk should have been the one place where they were equal. But even for all of the major female punk stars — Poly Styrene in X-Ray Spex, the Raincoats, and Pauline Murray of Penetration — it just wasn't.

In 1978, for instance, Blondie's record company actually ran a large display ad featuring Debbie Harry in a skimpy dress — below it the words: "WOULDN'T YOU LIKE TO RIP HER TO SHREDS?"

Seriously, they fucking did that.

The music industry media were just as bad. They'd focus on the clothing of female punk performers, or their looks, or they'd hit them with critical standards they didn't ever extend to guys in the scene. It was enough to make female punks want to spit. Or quit.

But Ari Up and the Slits — and the Punk Rock Virgins and Tit Sweat and others — wouldn't quit. If anything, they became even more determined to shake things up. So, they'd deliberately dress in rags, refuse to comb their hair, and generally refuse to behave like any of the female performers who'd gone before them.

Now, you might say that none of that was particularly new. Mama Cass and Janis Joplin hadn't been supermodels or paragons of virtue, either. But neither of them — nor any other female rock 'n' roll star that I could think of — had been as deliberately provocative and fearless as the female punks. They were the first to refuse to play along with the male-run, male-dominated rock game.

If punk was rebellion, then the women of punk were a rebellion within the genre itself. They were flipping the finger to society in a way that no one had ever done before. They'd found a way to break free of a lot of social conventions, especially the ones relating to femininity.

Anyway. That's my confession, on behalf of the entire subculture to which I belonged: the guys of punk should have been feminists, all the time.

But we weren't, not nearly enough.

CHAPTER 34

Inside the courtroom, Thomas M. Jones appeared bored as he stood between David Dennison and his associate, Mr. Popowich. Judge O'Sullivan looked at Jones over the top of his reading glasses.

"Do you understand the charges against you?" O'Sullivan asked.

Jones said nothing.

O'Sullivan's longtime clerk, Bobby Edwards, had read out the list of charges. There were the 121 charges of felony murder and the 311 counts of attempted murder. The names of the victims were read out, too, so Bobby had been reading for more than half an hour. He described charge after charge after charge found in the grand jury's indictment. He had started with a charge of "seditious conspiracy," which some considered a big deal. Namely, that Jones had "an intent to cause the overthrow or destruction of the lawful civil authority of these United States of America." That one, X told me, carried the death penalty.

But Jones's lawyers were likely not worried about the sedition charge. First, nobody ever got charged with sedition anymore, apparently. Second, sedition — like bribery — was a criminal act that generally required another participant to stick. And, as was well known, Thomas M. Jones had acted entirely alone.

But, more ominously, Edwards also announced that Jones had been charged with the murders of two federal law-enforcement officers, Glen and Cathy Beaupre. This was more problematic. The Beaupres were members of the United States Marshals Service and they had been dropping their four-year-old daughter, Tina, off at the daycare at the YWCA that morning. Tina had also been killed.

If he was found guilty of killing the Beaupres, he would definitely be given the death penalty.

Once again, X and I were standing at the back of the jam-packed courtroom. When the clerk finally read Nagamo's and Eddie's names, we looked at each other and said nothing. But when the clerk read out the rape charge — that, on the third day of November in the year 1975, in Clinton, Maine, Thomas M. Jones committed a gross sexual assault against a minor — Jones abruptly turned to scan the assembled crowd. There was a murmur as he did so. It was obvious he was looking for someone.

I wasn't planning on losing my cool, but I kind of did. "She isn't here, you prick," I hissed, and a few people turned to look at me. There was a small army of armed security guys in there, and a couple of them looked at me, too, frowning. They thought Jones was a prick, too, probably, so instead of arresting me, they just signaled for me to keep quiet.

X, however, was now staring at Jones, and Jones was staring right back at X. X's eyes had turned black, like they get when he's about to beat the living shit out of someone. A moment went by, then another. I half expected something to be said, or something to happen. But nothing did. Jones shifted his gaze back to Judge O'Sullivan, and the moment passed.

O'Sullivan addressed the defendant again. "Mr. Jones, do you understand the charges against you?"

There was silence, except for the sounds of reporters scribbling in their notebooks and people shifting in their seats, craning to get a better look.

O'Sullivan's scalp was getting noticeably redder. He squinted at the defense lawyer. "Mr. Dennison, does your client understand the charges against him?"

Dennison shrugged. "Your Honor, we have made many efforts to get our client to give us instructions," he said. "Some of have been successful, some have not."

A full minute went by. O'Sullivan regarded Dennison, then DA Martin at the prosecutor's table. O'Sullivan and Martin had both been expecting this moment to come. Dennison, they knew, almost certainly planned to argue that his client lacked the mental capacity to kill or rape anyone. It was the only way to avoid the death penalty. So, why wasn't he saying that his client was pleading insanity?

"Very well," Judge O'Sullivan finally said. "The accused is not indicating that he understands the charges against him, one way or another. So …" He paused to look down at a stack of papers in front of him. "On its own motion, then, this court possesses the jurisdiction to order that the defendant be examined by the State Forensic Service for evaluation of the defendant's competency to proceed. The court requires that the State Forensic Service shall promptly examine the defendant and report its initial determination regarding the defendant's competency to proceed to this court. A copy of the report should be filed by the State Forensic Service to Mr. Dennison and Ms. Martin. Is that understood?"

Dennison nodded his head, clearly pleased. "Yes, Your Honor."

The DA also nodded, not looking pleased at all. "Yes, Your Honor."

"Very well," O'Sullivan said, as he lowered his gavel. "I require this report in twenty-one days or less. Court is adjourned."

Thomas M. Jones was led away, scanning the courtroom as he left.

Maine Superior Court Justice Sean O'Sullivan glared at David Dennison.

DA Martin could see that O'Sullivan's scalp was turning an impressive red-pink color — never a good sign for an attorney who'd been summoned to O'Sullivan's chambers.

Directly behind Martin and Dennison, standing near stacks of *American Law Reports*, the assistant DAs and Dennison's assistants looked on silently.

If he noticed the imminent danger, Dennison gave no indication. His eyes were on the thin report in front of O'Sullivan. He pointed at it.

"So?" asked O'Sullivan.

"Dr. Fogel could not conclude if my client was fit to stand trial, Your Honor. He —"

Martin cut him off. "Nor did Dr. Fogel conclude that he *wasn't* fit to stand trial, Mr. Dennison." The lawyer gave her a dirty look. "He couldn't reach any conclusion after meeting with your client three times."

Dennison was unmoved. "My client has a constitutional right to remain silent. But you cannot infer from that silence, Miss Martin, that my client possesses the requisite ability to instruct his legal counsel or to participate in a complex and onerous criminal proceeding."

"It's Ms., not Miss, Mr. Dennison," Martin said. "And silence does not equal insanity."

There was pause and Justice O'Sullivan took advantage of it. "Your client may not have said a word to Dr. Fogel or anyone else in the State Forensic Service, Mr. Dennison, but there is no shortage of words in his manifesto, or autobiography, or whatever the hell it is. There are plenty of words in there. And none of them suggest that your client in any way possesses a mental disease or defect and therefore lacked the capacity to appreciate the wrongfulness of the criminal conduct he is accused of."

Dennison raised his manicured hands in protest. "Your Honor, you know our position on Mr. Jones's diary," he said, eyes closed as if in prayer. "We take the position that the document the FBI seized was a lengthy letter to me and my colleague Mr. Popowich, and therefore protected by attorney-client privilege ..."

O'Sullivan slapped the top of his desk. "I know what your argument is, Mr. Dennison!" he snapped. "I've read your motion and supporting materials. We will deal with that issue when your motion is heard. In the meantime, all of us have a dilemma. Even you."

Dennison arched a sculpted eyebrow. "Even me? How so?"

"Because, Mr. Dennison," O'Sullivan leaned back in his chair and locked his hands behind his head, "if your client lacks capacity, he lacks capacity to instruct counsel. And if he isn't instructing counsel, I'm not entirely sure what you and Mr. Popowich are still doing here in my chambers. Are you just *pretending* to know what is in your client's best interest, Mr. Dennison?"

Dennison, momentarily caught off-guard, stammered, "Of course not, Your Honor! Even if our client is indeed insane, we still have an obligation to mount a vigorous defense. That is our obligation as officers of the court, isn't it?"

"Mr. Dennison," O'Sullivan said after a long pause, "the general principle is that you cannot take on a client who lacks the capacity to give you instructions. The only time you can do that is when you are appointed by the court.... And I don't recall appointing you to represent Mr. Jones. You and your associate flew up here from New York City to do that, Mr. Dennison, all on your own. I think you broke the sound barrier to get here before some other publicity-seeking defense attorney could do so."

David Dennison remained uncharacteristically silent.

"I am not of the view that your client lacks the capacity to stand trial, Mr. Dennison," Justice O'Sullivan said finally. But before Dennison could open his mouth to protest, the judge held up a hand and turned his gaze on DA Martin. "That said, I am equally not convinced that the manuscript should not be excluded. It is more than highly prejudicial — it is arguably protected by attorney-client privilege, Ms. Martin. You know the rules."

Martin looked uncharacteristically shocked. She had obviously not been expecting this. David Dennison, also visibly surprised by this unexpected turn of events, suppressed a smile.

"I will hear your arguments on the motion to exclude the manuscript on Monday," O'Sullivan said, squinting at his calendar and waving a hand at the assembled attorneys. "That will be all for today."

CHAPTER 35

Just as the first one had, X's latest column in *Creem* resulted in several hastily arranged meetings — this one in the office of Portland's police chief. In attendance were Savoie, Laverty, the DA, and two assistant DAs. And, of course, Chief Chow.

Everyone looked pissed off, except Chow, who never seemed to lose his cool, Laverty noticed.

Savoie held up the offending issue, clearly furious. "This is a serious breach, Chief. Who leaked this information to this frigging kid? This is a disgrace!"

Nobody disagreed. They were all reading, or rereading, the column.

The headline was bad enough: "ACCUSED PORTLAND BOMBER MAY WALK, SOURCE SAYS."

But the column itself, from the perspective of the police and prosecutors present, was way, way worse. It was written in X's usual detached style. Not too many adjectives, no verbal overkill, but lots of stuff that would leave the reader shocked.

Accused Portland bomber Thomas M. Jones may walk, sources tell *Creem*'s Non-Conformist News Agency.

Jones's publicity-loving New York City attorney, David Dennison, may succeed in stopping prosecutors from using Jones's "manifesto" against him in the trial, where Jones is facing more than one hundred counts of first-degree murder. Sources who spoke on the condition that they would not be identified told *Creem* that the Maine Superior Court judge overseeing the case is likely to agree that the manifesto should be excluded because it is protected by attorney-client privilege.

In the three-hundred-page manifesto, Jones describes in great detail his plans to bomb the Portland YWCA, and his hatred of women and minorities. But the document is apparently written in the form of a letter to Dennison and his law firm on Broadway in NYC.

In Maine and most American states, communications between attorneys and their clients can't be used in court. And if Jones's rambling, angry manuscript is excluded in the case, sources told us, Jones may walk on all of the bombing-related charges.

There is only one eyewitness, Portland security guard Bob Cox, who is ready to testify

> that he *may have seen* Jones near the YWCA on the morning of April 13, 1981. Cox suffered a head injury in the bombing, however, and may be considered an unreliable witness.
>
> Any of the other evidence gathered is circumstantial, sources say. The bomber did not leave behind a single fingerprint or any other incriminating evidence. Without the manuscript — and without a solid eyewitness who can place him at the scene — the prosecution against Jones, led by Portland District Attorney Sharon Martin, will collapse, the source said.
>
> If the hundreds of bomb-related charges Jones is facing are dismissed, only a four-year-old rape charge against Jones could be left to prosecute, *Creem* has been told. The name of the victim is being withheld by *Creem* to protect her identity.

Laverty looked up from the magazine. "How nice," she said. "He wants to protect the identity of his friend, but he doesn't want to protect the case we have against Jones."

The DA was also pissed. She turned to her two assistant DAs. "We need to consider charging X and *Creem* with contempt," she said. "This article will have Dennison seeking a mistrial before the trial even gets underway …"

Chow, who had been waiting for them to finish reading, held up a hand. “If you do that, the press will rally around this young man and argue that you are violating their First Amendment rights,” he said, his voice even. “We all know what he has written here is true. If the manuscript is excluded, the bombing case could collapse.”

“We still have Bob Cox and the employees at the truck rental place in Vermont,” one of the assistant DAs said, vainly trying to sound hopeful.

“Cox was knocked cold by the bomb and hasn’t worked since,” Laverty said, shaking her head. “Have you guys interviewed him recently? He can’t remember what he had for breakfast most days. He’s under psychiatric care and it seems he’ll be a less-than-ideal eyewitness.”

Martin chimed in. “And the truck rental guys in Vermont didn’t have security cameras, and none of them remember much about Jones. None of them definitively picked him out of the lineup. Dennison will make mincemeat of them.”

“So, what do we do, folks?” Savoie asked. “Do we just let this punk reporter wreck months of police work?”

Chow shook his head. “Detective, the entire case was largely dependent on the admissibility of the manuscript long before X wrote his article.”

Just then the phone on Chow’s desk rang. He picked it up and listened. “Yes,” he said, three times, and then hung up. He looked up at Martin and her assistant DAs.

"That was Justice O'Sullivan's clerk," he said. "Apparently his daughter is a fan of X's and has a subscription to *Creem*. She showed him the article this morning." Chow paused. "The judge would like to see all of you in his chambers right away. He's very angry, but I suspect all of you figured that out already."

CHAPTER 36

The first blow, Sister Betty said, came as she was rounding the corner — a punch to her left ear, not super hard but hard enough.

She'd been taking a shortcut, walking from Congress Street toward Gary's, doing some errands and heading to a get-together of the X Gang. She'd just stepped into the alleyway that ran parallel to Free Street and was getting close to Gary's when it happened.

It was so sudden, and so unexpected, at first she thought she might have walked into a board protruding from a garbage bin or something. But, as she was bent over, swearing and clutching the side of her head, she saw the three pairs of boots on the asphalt in front of her.

The boots were attached to three of the four guys who had been at Gary's on the night of the Hot Nasties gig.

Sister Betty lurched back from them, shocked. They were all wearing jeans, jean jackets, Timberland boots, and flannel shirts. Typical jock wear. They were all smirking at her.

"Well, well, well," the short, stocky one she remembered said in a nasal twang. He sounded like he was from somewhere else — mid-coast, maybe? Lots of dropped *R*s and weird pronunciations. "'Chupta, girl?"

"You fucking hit me!" Sister Betty said, her initial shock replaced with anger. "What the fuck?"

"You're a spleeny one, ain't cha?" Short Stocky said, grinning. "Sensitive little bitch." He and his friends laughed.

Sister Betty paused, clutching her throbbing ear, considering her options. It was midafternoon on a Saturday, but absolutely no one else was around. She had to focus on not getting beaten to death, so she kept quiet.

"Ayuh," Short Stocky said, which Sister Betty took to mean yes. "Ain't nobody around 'cept you and us, girlie." He paused, pointing down at the plastic Electric Buddha record bag she was carrying. "You get us a present?"

Before she could say anything or react, Short Stocky snatched away the bag and peered inside. He extracted the Slits LP, which had cost Sister Betty twenty bucks — a lot of money.

"*Return of the Giant Slits*," Short Stocky read, examining the cover, then turned it over. He held it up for his two pals to see. "Look like fuckin' dykes, don't they, fellas?" His two friends nodded, laughing.

Short Stocky stepped toward the brick wall and smashed the record against it. He then folded the record in two and tossed it to the ground. "It's clutch now," he said. "Sorry, dyke."

Sister Betty, now afraid, considered whether she would be able to run away fast enough. She decided that she couldn't.

In the pocket of her leather jacket was a small Swiss Army knife. With the three thugs closely watching her for a reaction, she knew she'd never get to the knife in time — and, even if she did, one of them would be more likely to use it against her.

Short Stocky stepped closer, close enough that she could smell his bad breath. She didn't want to cry, but she felt that she might.

"You kinda look like a dyke yourself, dyke," Short Stocky hissed. He reached up and pushed her shoulder, hard. Sister Betty stumbled back, but she didn't fall over. "You a dyke?" he said, stepping toward her.

"Leave me alone. There's three of you and just one of me ..."

Short Stocky turned to his pals and laughed. "And you think a little *dite* like you could take one of us?" he said, using the coaster word that means "a tiny amount."

Sister Betty said nothing, easing her right hand into her jacket pocket. Short Stocky didn't seem to notice.

"You need to tell your dyke friend in that fag band ... what are they called, Billy?" he asked, turning to one of the other two, the taller one.

"The Hot Nasties," Billy said.

"Oh yeah, the fag Nasties," Short Stocky said, pointing at Sister Betty, his finger an inch from her face. "You need to tell that dyke drummer that we know who she is and that she deserved what she got. And that she needs to drop out of that trial now."

"Why?" Sister Betty said, genuinely bewildered.

"Because she can fuck it all up, that's why!" He was yelling now and stepping closer. "The bomber will walk because of her!"

Sister Betty did not understand, at all, how anyone could possibly reach that conclusion. The complete reverse was true: if Thomas M. Jones somehow escaped prosecution for the murders, it was only the remaining rape charge that would send him to prison.

But Betty didn't bother to argue: the three thugs who had attacked her were idiots. Instead of saying anything, she pulled out the Swiss Army knife, quickly pried open the four-inch blade, and slashed at Short Stocky. A gash opened up on the top of his hand, and the blood started to flow.

"You bitch!" he screamed over and over.

At that point, there was little doubt the three of them would have jumped Sister Betty and hurt her badly — even killed her. But X and I had heard Short Stocky yelling as far away as Congress Street and came running. We used the same shortcut to get to Gary's pretty often, too.

In an instant, X had a short length of lead pipe in his fist. I reached down to pick up a brick from beside a Dumpster. It didn't take long.

We stopped only when we started to hear sirens.

The three guys were alive, but they lay crumpled on the ground, unconscious — or close to it — and bleeding all over the place. X, me, and Sister Betty took off and jogged the rest of the way to Gary's and went in the back way.

We never saw Short Stocky and his friends again.

CHAPTER 37

Judge O'Sullivan, as Chief Chow had warned them, was pissed. *Really* pissed.

From his perch behind the big wooden desk in courtroom one, he glared down at the DA and the prosecution teams. The chief and FBI special agent Theresa Laverty sat behind them in the front row of benches. Nobody said a word. None of them moved a muscle.

O'Sullivan's clerk, Bobby Edwards, sat rigid as a stone to O'Sullivan's left.

X's column in the newest issue of *Creem* magazine had likely been read by all of the big-shot reporters in the major newspapers and TV networks, but so far none of them were reporting on it. But that hadn't mitigated any of Justice O'Sullivan's anger.

"Can anyone explain to me how confidential matters that were discussed in my chambers found their way into this … this … rag?" O'Sullivan said, waving a copy of *Creem* in the air. Laverty noticed that the cover featured a picture of Debbie Harry and Chris Stein of Blondie.

As O'Sullivan had asked the question a half-dozen times, in a half-dozen different ways — each attempt eliciting silence from the assembled group — the judge's scalp became progressively redder. Laverty thought that O'Sullivan was edging perilously close to having a stroke.

O'Sullivan then focused his attention on Jones's lawyer, who he clearly regarded as the likely culprit. "Mr. Dennison," he said, his voice low and menacing, "leaking such information to the media would be an excellent way to obtain a mistrial, wouldn't it?"

Dennison leapt to his feet, arms and hands gesturing in all directions, like a marionette in a fancy suit. He looked completely panicked. O'Sullivan may be a judge in what Dennison probably regarded as an inbred judicial backwater, but Dennison must have known that O'Sullivan was no fool, either, and not ever to be trifled with. He stammered and waved his hands.

"Your Honor, under no circumstances would the defense ever do such a thing!" He looked over at his assistant, who had suddenly taken considerable interest in the pattern of the wood grain on the defense table. "My associates and I would never leak such information to the media —"

O'Sullivan cut him off with the wave of a hand. "Oh, really?" he said. "I had been under the impression that you and your associates were entirely too fond of your press clippings, Mr. Dennison. Was I mistaken in that?"

Laverty raised a hand to her mouth to hide a smile.

Dennison's response was characteristically cocky. "Your Honor, it would not be in the interest of the defense to seek a mistrial in a prosecution in which we expect to be successful," he said, regaining some of his composure. "As you know, we are ready to argue the merits of our motion to exclude Mr. Jones's privileged communications. And we expect to be successful on that motion."

"So, this magazine article claims," O'Sullivan said, holding it up again, "that they know all about your defense strategy, Mr. Dennison. I find that most interesting."

Dennison looked distraught. "Your Honor, I swear to you as an officer of the court that we did not communicate in any way with this person, whoever they are. We want to win in court, not in the media."

"That'd be a first," O'Sullivan said dryly. He then turned his attention to the District Attorney. "Ms. Martin."

The DA rose slowly to her feet. "Yes, Your Honor."

"Do you know the person who wrote this article?"

"Yes, Your Honor, I do." She held up a thumb and pointed in the direction of Laverty. "I believe my colleague here from the FBI, as well as many in the Portland PD, are familiar with him, as well."

"And you have dealt with this individual before?" O'Sullivan asked.

"Yes, Your Honor," she said. "Unfortunately."

"Why 'unfortunately,' Ms. Martin?"

"Because, Your Honor, this ... this young man is —"

O'Sullivan cut her off. "Young? How young is he?"

Martin turned to look at Laverty, who shrugged, maintaining her courageous silence. "Not certain, Your Honor," she said. "But I would think he is in his early twenties. I believe he's in his first year of the journalism program at the University of Southern Maine ..."

"Wait a damn minute. Are you telling me that this person who has found out highly confidential details about what is arguably the most important criminal trial in the recent history of the United States is ... what? A kid, barely out of high school? Is that what you're telling me?"

The DA scanned the top of the table, searching for the right words. She came up with nothing. "He is a very resourceful young man, Your Honor," she said. "He also has an unusually developed knowledge of the extreme right ..."

"He is apparently far more 'resourceful' than many of the attorneys who appear before me!" O'Sullivan hollered, slapping the magazine down on his desk. He glared at the DA. "Ms. Martin, I think I need to meet this person." He tilted his head and looked at Laverty and Chow. "Would the FBI or the Portland Police Department have any difficulty in locating this person? Would that be too much trouble?"

Laverty and the chief stood up simultaneously.

"Your Honor, I would recommend against it," Chow said, calm and cool as ever. "This young man is highly intelligent and will never, under any circumstances, reveal his sources. He's already quoted the First Amendment to me, in my office."

O'Sullivan thought about that for a few moments. "There's no harm in trying, is there, Chief?" he asked. "All of us have an interest in ensuring that justice is done in this case, do we not?"

"Yes, of course, Your Honor," said Chow. "But I again caution against letting this young man turn this very important prosecution into a First Amendment cause célèbre."

"This isn't my first rodeo, Chief. I have no intention in letting that happen. But I still want him brought here before me. Understood?"

Laverty and Savoie nodded and hustled out of courtroom one.

CHAPTER 38

When they tracked him down at his folks' place, X was typically unfazed. Standing at the front door — me looking over one shoulder, his attorney dad over the other — X fastened his uneven pupils on Laverty and Savoie. They told him Judge O'Sullivan would like to speak with him. X looked bored, like he'd been expecting it.

"Wait a second." X's dad stepped forward. "Do you have a bench warrant or a summons?"

"No," Laverty said. "We came directly from the courthouse. We have no summons or warrant."

"So, this is more of a request than a demand, then?"

Savoie shrugged. "I suppose so. We could probably get a summons. But we think everyone wants to avoid that. The judge just wants to have a talk with your son … about the column he wrote."

X's dad crossed his arms over his Montreal Canadiens T-shirt. "So, let me get this straight. A superior court judge wants to have a chit-chat with my son about his article, and we're not supposed to think that's significant." Neither Laverty or Savoie responded. "If he agrees, I'm coming with him," he added. "He needs representation."

Savoie shrugged. "The judge didn't say you couldn't come," he said. "He just said he wanted your son to come."

We all looked at X to see if he was going to refuse to go. My money was on him refusing, personally.

"I'll go," he finally said.

"Fine," X's dad said. "I'll get changed. Can you give us a few minutes, please?"

"No problem," Savoie said. "We'll wait."

"You're welcome to wait inside, officers," X's dad said.

"That's okay," Savoie said, looking uncomfortable. "We'll wait in the car."

X's dad closed the door. "You sure about this?" he asked. "You're under no obligation to go, you know."

X shrugged. "I'm not concerned. It'll give me more material for my next column, if nothing else."

X's dad laughed, then looked at me.

"I'm coming, too," I said, before anyone could say I wasn't.

X's dad smiled and put a hand on my shoulder. "I expected nothing less, Kurt."

Judge O'Sullivan squinted over the top of his reading glasses at X. Everyone in the courtroom looked nervous, especially the judge's clerk, Bobby Edwards. I watched him out of the corner of my eye. The clerk was doing his very best to render himself invisible, to avoid the gaze of his boss, me, or X, who he had foolishly agreed to speak to in exchange for a few free beers. So he kept reading and rereading the same paragraph in his well-thumbed copy of the *Maine Rules of Court*.

X and his dad — now sporting a jacket and tie — were sitting across from Edwards, at the DA's table. DA Martin and her assistant DAs had been very happy to relinquish the table, so Justice O'Sullivan could get mad at someone else for a change. They were now seated in the first row. Jones's lawyer, David Dennison, was there, too, along with his assistant. Both were watching the exchange with great interest.

I, meanwhile, sat between the two groups of attorneys, slouched on the uncomfortable wooden pew. I looked at Judge O'Sullivan, the only judge those of us in the X Gang had ever encountered, really. He had presided over the trial of the skinheads who had killed our friends. That trial had been a total train wreck, but O'Sullivan had left the X Gang with the impression that he possessed a certain amount of integrity and intelligence. To us, most members of the establishment usually lacked both.

At the moment Justice O'Sullivan was evaluating X, apparently trying to figure out how to get him to talk without, among other things, turning their little informal chit-chat into a full-blown First Amendment constitutional challenge. Which, according to X's dad, they were quite prepared to do.

The judge tried again. "Young man, I don't think I have to tell you how critically important this trial is," he said, his voice low. "One hundred and twenty-one men, women, and children were killed in the Portland YWCA bombing, and three times that number were critically hurt." He paused. "I understand you even had two friends among the dead?"

I could see X's profile and could tell he was clenching his jaw. But he remained silent.

"You have a constitutional right to write what you please," O'Sullivan continued. "But reasonable limits have been placed on that, to ensure that the constitutional rights of Mr. Jones, and others, are protected."

X finally spoke, his voice quiet. "What about the constitutional rights of a rape victim?" he said, staring at O'Sullivan.

"You know that I cannot discuss individuals, particularly on the eve of trial, son," O'Sullivan said quickly. "The allegations with respect to Ms. Jett are just that, for now. Allegations."

X said nothing.

"Can you tell me how you came to be in possession of the information you disclosed in your article?" the judge asked for the third time.

"No," X said.

"Statements made in a judge's chambers are highly confidential, you know," O'Sullivan said, trying again.

"What you published can have an impact on the trial. I possess the authority to have you held in contempt, young man."

X's dad started to say something, but X interrupted. "I know you do," he said, "but the minute you do, it will prove what I wrote was true."

"What do you mean?"

"None of the regular media are following up on what I wrote," X said, crossing his arms. "But they definitely will if you throw me in a cell."

The judge stared at him, marveling at his arrogance or his intelligence. Or both. "Perhaps," he said. "But perhaps a bit of time cooling your heels in a cell will persuade you to co-operate with the court."

X's dad tried to ease the tension. "You don't know my son, Your Honor," he said. "His mother and I can tell you that grounding him hasn't ever worked. It makes him even more stubborn."

At that, Judge O'Sullivan actually laughed, then everyone else did, too — except X, of course. He just sat there, arms crossed, expressionless.

"Yes, my daughters are like that," the judge said, smiling. "I think I know what you mean." He then made a point of frowning, as if trying to regain control. "But your son must appreciate the difficulty he has created for this court."

If he did, X didn't acknowledge it. Instead, he decided to turn Justice O'Sullivan's interrogation of him into an interview of Justice O'Sullivan. He looked directly at the judge and asked, "So, is it true that you are prepared to keep the DA from using the killer's confession in the trial?"

The judge blinked several times, then said carefully, "Son, you know quite well, I think, that I am not permitted to answer any such question outside the context of the trial. Until I do so, any document offered by either side is just paper. It is just words."

X nodded. "Words," he said, with emphasis. "Words have power."

O'Sullivan's frown deepened. "I'm sorry. I'm afraid I don't understand your point."

X pointed a thumb at David Dennison and his assistant. "That's what they want to argue," he said, "that words are just words. That they don't matter."

Justice O'Sullivan must have known, at some level, that he should not be drawn into a protracted back and forth with this rather odd young man with the long hair and the earring and the punk rock outfit. But he was anyway.

"What is your point, young man?" he asked, as if genuinely curious.

"All of what happened that day in April," X said, one hand up a bit, sort of looking like a preacher or something. "Everything that has happened since. Even everything that is happening here today." He paused. "It is all about words," X continued. "Words have power. Words were what found the killer, and shaped him, and sent him out to kill all those people. Not a person.

Just words on a page." X paused, waiting for the judge to stop him, perhaps. But O'Sullivan didn't stop him. "Words are all that he cares about. They're everything to him. If you eliminate the words, if you exclude the book he wrote — and if you ignore the other book, the one that changed him — you will be left with nothing. And he will go free."

Judge O'Sullivan looked at Dennison. He had probably expected the lawyer to object to what X was saying. But none of it was on the record. The questioning of the *Creem* magazine writer was a bit like a voir dire — where the admissibility of a witness's evidence is considered in the absence of the jury. Except it wasn't voir dire. And X wasn't even a witness. It was ... off the record, I guess.

So, Dennison wisely kept quiet.

I knew at that point that X wasn't going to be thrown in a jail cell, and that O'Sullivan wasn't going to get X to spill the beans on Bobby Edwards, either. Edwards probably sensed it, too, because he looked as if he had started to breathe again.

"Words turned him into a killer," X said, "and who he wanted to kill, more than anything, were *women*."

CHAPTER 39

The hearing to present the motion to prevent the prosecution from relying on Thomas M. Jones's manuscript got started on a Monday morning in courtroom one. Initially, Judge O'Sullivan — likely concerned about the sort of mistrial-inducing journalism X had indulged in — had wanted to exclude the media from attending the hearing. But when a trio of lawyers from the *New York Times* filed an emergency motion to permit reporters to attend, O'Sullivan gave up trying to manage the media. Reporters would be permitted to cover David Dennison's motion.

X and I were there, along with a horde of print, TV, and radio reporters, and a crowd of other citizens who had lined up early to get a seat. While the attorneys scrutinized their papers and spoke to each other in whispers, everyone else was watching Thomas M. Jones.

Four burly courthouse security officers surrounded the prisoner. But the likelihood of Jones making a run for it was pretty small. He was chained at his wrists and feet. His head had been shaven while he was in custody, and it made him look older, less like an all-American boy. Weeks in a cell in solitary confinement had erased the tan he'd had when he was arrested on the banks of the Androscoggin River. He looked less fit, too. The muscular, lean Thomas M. Jones from his aborted bail hearing had given way to a slightly gaunt look.

"All rise!" Bobby Edwards called out abruptly as Judge O'Sullivan walked briskly through the door with a "NO ADMITTANCE" sign on it. We all rose, Jones included. O'Sullivan stepped up to the elevated platform on which his desk and chair had been placed and sat down. He invited everyone else to do the same.

"Good morning, everyone," he said. He looked over at Jones, who was staring straight ahead. "Good morning, Ms. Martin and Mr. Dennison. Good morning to the accused, as well."

Jones nodded but didn't say anything. The guards around Jones glared at him, looking like they wanted to kill him on the spot.

O'Sullivan nodded in the direction of Dennison, who looked freshly barbered and shaved, ready for his close-up. "If you are ready, Mr. Dennison, you may proceed."

Dennison stood, buttoned his double-breasted jacket, smoothed his hair, which didn't need smoothing, and gave a confident smile. "Good morning, Your Honor." He nodded his perfectly coiffed head in the direction of the District Attorney and her assistant DAs. "Good morning to the District Attorney and the court."

He looked down at the sheets of paper on the lectern but I got the impression he knew this argument cold. "Your Honor, we are here today to take the position that the letter Mr. Jones wrote is subject to attorney-client privilege and should therefore not be admissible as evidence by the prosecution." Dennison's velvet tones washed over the courtroom. "The law, in this regard, is well settled and has been clear from the beginnings of these American states: the confidential communications between an attorney and his accused client cannot be disclosed or used against the accused. Under any circumstances. Ever."

From where we were sitting, I could see the DA frowning as she scribbled away on a yellow legal notepad.

Dennison continued, "Attorney-client privilege is one of the oldest privileges known to our system, Your Honor, and for good reason. No less than the U.S. Supreme Court has held that attorney-client privilege assures confidentiality and helps accused persons make full and frank disclosure to their legal counsel. In that way, we are able to represent our clients and give them candid advice."

Dennison reached to the side of the lectern and picked up a thick stack of papers. Jaw squared, expression firm, the lawyer held it up long enough to ensure that the media sketch artists would be able to capture the dramatic moment. "This," Dennison said finally, "this document is indisputably protected by attorney-client privilege. It bears those words at the top of the very first page: 'PROTECTED BY ATTORNEY-CLIENT PRIVILEGE'. Below that, Your Honor, it reads, 'DEAR MR. DENNISON.'"

He paused for dramatic effect, but it wasn't really necessary. It already *was* dramatic: if that was what it said, and that was what attorney-client privilege meant, then — to my legally untrained ears, at least — the DA was fucked. Without quoting any cases or statutes or any of that crap, David Dennison already seemed to be winning.

Dennison looked at the judge, who had his head bent over his desk and was scribbling away. To lawyers, X's dad had told us, this was always a good sign. It meant the judge was listening and was taking note. Literally.

"Those words were written by Mr. Jones," Dennison said, returning the manuscript to its spot beside the lectern. He picked up another thinner document. "And we have three reports by handwriting analysts who attest to the fact that those critically important words were written by Mr. Jones and no other person. I submit those reports as exhibits one, two, and three."

Dennison's assistant walked over to Bobby Edwards and gave him the reports from the handwriting experts. He then walked to DA Martin's table and with a big, cocky smile that could not be seen by the judge, he handed her the reports, too.

"The exhibits are so entered," O'Sullivan said. "Exhibits one, two, and three."

It was going to be a long day for the prosecution.

CHAPTER 40

Special Agent Laverty reread the letter several times. The two prison guards on duty had found it on the bed beside the body of Thomas M. Jones. In Jones's hand was a stamped, self-addressed envelope addressed to a Mr. John Smith.

Dear John, the letter read,

> *Thank you for your many letters. They have been very thoughtful and insightful. As I am sure you know, I am very limited by what I can say. The Maine Department of Corrections looks at all of my mail, and I presume they will look at this letter, too. But as I am sure you also know, words are very important to me. When I was younger, books were my best friends. They were my life. When I read* The Patriot Diaries, *I was given my life's mission. It gave me my path.*

I must be very careful about what I say about the issue you have been raising with me in your letters. Suffice to say that, when I learned what was happening there — when I learned about the abortuary, a slaughterhouse for the unborn, a war on boys and men — I could not look away. I could not ignore the blood being spilled there.

Words, at a certain point, are not enough. Words must be transformed into action.

I cannot say more, Mr. Smith, but I again thank you for your kindness and fraternal friendship. We will see each other soon, I hope.

Sincerely

The letter had been left unsigned.

Laverty picked up one of the letters addressed to Jones that had been entered into evidence.

Dear Thomas,

We have been following your trial and struggle in the news media, which always gives a slanted and distorted picture of what is going on. Despite that, we know the truth: you have been a soldier in the struggle to preserve the rights and dignity of men.

Like you, we believe in men going their own way. Those like us will not surrender our will to the social expectations of women and society, because both have become hostile against masculinity. To feminazis, for all intents and purposes, our kind of man does not exist. An urbanite might keep to his own apartment, while some men like us may simply head into the wilderness and go off the grid.

We understand that is what you did, and we greatly admire you for it. If you want to talk about your experience in the glorious and solitary wilderness, please use the enclosed envelope.

Yours sincerely,
John Smith

X and I were in the Upchuck sisters' basement. I was on the old couch with Patti and Sister Betty. X was standing over by the old drum kit and amps, looking down into a box marked "DEPARTMENT OF CHEMISTRY, UNIVERSITY OF SOUTHERN MAINE."

"He's really dead?" Sister Betty said, sitting on the edge of the couch, looking a bit pale. "You're sure?"

X didn't look at her. He was still looking inside the box. "Yes," he said. "It's not on the news yet. But there are lots of ambulances and cops on Federal Street. They've cordoned off the courthouse."

"How do you know?" she asked. She was leaning forward, her knees tightly together and her hands clasped on top of her knees.

"My dad," X said. "He was in the courthouse library when word started to spread. He called me."

"Did he commit suicide?" Sister Betty asked.

X looked right at her. "He didn't commit suicide, Betty."

"Good riddance," Patti said. She was smiling, happy. "This is awesome! Whoever did this deserves a fucking award."

"Right," X said, his face blank.

Patti may have been happy, but I wasn't. Sister Betty didn't look like she was, either.

Patti looked at the rest of us, frowning. "I don't know why the rest of you look so morose. I think this calls for a toast," she said, standing up. "Who wants an RC Cola? Kurt? Betty?"

I said sure. Betty nodded. Patti left to get the drinks from upstairs.

X waited until she was gone, then walked over to Sister Betty and crouched down in front of her. She avoided his eyes. "Betty," he said.

She didn't respond.

He said her name again and put one hand on her shoulder.

When she finally looked up, she looked scared. I slid over and put an arm around her shoulders. She avoided our eyes but started speaking in a low monotone. "I couldn't take it anymore. All the death and destruction he caused. The little kids he killed. Eddie and Nagamo. The women and girls. Jessie …" She paused, and her body heaved, like she was going to throw up. "So much youth, wasted."

We waited.

"It was easy," she said. "I just started writing him letters, talking about hating women. I knew that was what made him do it, from what Jessie told me."

"Using that typewriter?" X said, softly, indicating the one against the wall. The one the Punk Rock Virgins used to hammer out their song lyrics.

Sister Betty nodded.

"Kurt and I will get rid of it tonight," X said. "But ..."

"Don't worry," Sister Betty said. "I wore gloves when I wrote the letters. The envelopes I sent him were addressed to a P.O. box that doesn't exist. And I sprayed the tops of the stamps with this sealant, so the postal cancellation marks wouldn't stick. So, they won't know where the letters came from." She glanced up at X but quickly looked away. "I didn't need him to mail anything to John Smith. I just needed him to try."

X had told me what he suspected before we got there, but I still didn't understand how she'd done it. Couldn't really believe she'd done it at all, actually.

"Sister, how ...?"

"Over there," she said, pointing at the box in the corner marked "DEPARTMENT OF CHEMISTRY, UNIVERSITY OF SOUTHERN MAINE. TTX." She gave a tiny smile. "'TTX' doesn't just stand for 'True to X.' Sorry."

We paused and listened to the footsteps above us. Her sister was still upstairs in the kitchen, but she'd be back down soon.

"TTX," Sister Betty said, like she had been preparing for this moment. "A bit of it was in the box from my dad's lab. TTX is from this cute little fish, the puffer fish. They carry a super-deadly neurotoxin called tetrodotoxin. It's in their livers and skin."

We said nothing. I was in shock, I think.

"TTX weakens and then paralyzes muscles, really fast," she said. "It hits the respiratory system and kills you in less than an hour. It's a thousand times more poisonous than cyanide." She paused. "There's enough TTX in one puffer fish to kill thirty adult humans. There's no antidote."

"How did you get him to ingest it?" I whispered.

Sister Betty shrugged. "Just a few drops on the sticky part of the envelopes and on the stamps," she said. "It doesn't have a color or smell when it dries out. The second he licked the envelope or stamp to respond to John Smith, he was already dead."

X looked into Sister Betty's eyes, which were still scared. He squeezed her arm. "Kurt and I will get rid of the typewriter and the chemicals," he said, his voice low. "No one will ever know."

Sister Betty nodded. X stood up, just as we heard Patti coming down the basement stairs.

"You did the right thing," he said. "We'll protect you." He paused for the briefest moment. "Now, none of us will ever talk about this again. You got it?"

"No words?" she said.

"No words."

CHAPTER 41

Naturally, the cops and the FBI suspected X and me killed that bastard Jones. I mean, when all else fails, blame a punk, right?

For months, FBI special agent Laverty and Detective Savoie harangued and harassed me and X. They followed us around. They talked to our families. They "interviewed" us and then "interviewed" us again.

But they didn't suspect Sister Betty. Not once. Not a bit.

A big inquiry determined that the alleged Portland bomber had indeed been poisoned by person or persons who had sent letters to him, posing as fans. A rare and toxic poison had been applied to the part of the enclosed return envelopes, where someone would typically lick and seal it. The poison was hard to get, the inquiry determined, but not impossible. Any university zoology or botany student would be able to get their hands on the stuff.

The inquiry recommended that the deadly fish poison thereafter be subject to strict controls and disclosure.

But that was closing the proverbial barn door after the horse had left, I said to X. He nodded.

The inquiry also found not a trace of any clue — no fingerprints, no hair, no tissue, nothing — on the outside or the inside of the envelopes. Zero, zippo, zilch. All of the letters had been composed on a single Olivetti typewriter, they concluded. But they didn't know where the typewriter was.

I did. We did, I mean. It was at the bottom of Casco Bay, where X and I had deposited it. We'd borrowed Luke's dad's little tin fishing boat, and we tossed it over the side the same night Sister Betty confessed to us.

Splash!

But Laverty was smart. Once the inside and outside of the letters and the envelopes yielded nothing, Laverty looked at something else: the words.

The words used in those fake fan letters to Thomas M. Jones revealed a certain style, a certain way with words, dexterity with the language, you might say.

Her suspicion, therefore, landed on X and me. Both of us were writers, or at least aspiring writers. X in the pages of *Creem* and, before that, the *Non-Conformist News Agency* in high school. Me in the diary pages that you now clutch in your hands. She put together a team of linguists and English professors to analyze stuff that X and I had written and compare it to the letters sent to Thomas M. Jones.

The experts and the eggheads scrutinized punctuation. They considered grammar and spelling. They peered at sentence structure and spacing and choice of words. All of that crap. Their conclusion: the same person had written all of the letters. But that person was "unlikely to highly unlikely" to be either X or me.

In the final "interview" at Portland police HQ, Laverty was compelled to disclose this to me and X. We were represented at that point by X's dad, who had threatened to launch a massive lawsuit against the FBI and assorted police agencies if they didn't stop harassing us, as he put it.

Laverty had stared across the boardroom table at us, clearly incensed. Savoie, hunched beside her, scowled.

"Well, Agent Laverty and Detective Savoie, it would seem that you have failed in every one of your attempts to implicate my son and Kurt," X's dad said. "Can we conclude that your investigation of the boys is now finished?"

Laverty stirred. "Yes," she said, her lips barely moving.

"And there will be no further demands for interviews?"

"No."

"And you will provide me with the letter that I previously raised with you, declaring that neither my son nor Kurt are suspects in this homicide, in any way, shape, or form?" Our lawyer was clearly enjoying himself.

There was a long pause before Laverty finally spoke. "Yes," she almost hissed, "we will provide an exculpatory statement."

"Thank you, Special Agent," he said, sounding triumphant, as he got up to leave. X and I were already standing. "We wish you the best in your investigation and look forward to receiving your letter. Good day."

And with that, we walked out of Portland police headquarters. We never went back. At least, I didn't, anyway. X — having graduated from MSU and now duly employed as an actual, real, honest-to-god roving investigative journalist for various publications, *Rolling Stone* (god forbid) among them — may have gone back to interview cops about other cases. But me? I never went back. Never needed rehab again either. Not long after we got the letter from the FBI, I came out of the closet. At that point, tempting chemicals became less tempting to me; apart from the occasional beer, I virtually became straight edge, like X.

Hearing that I was glad to be gay, like Tom Robinson proudly sang, my dad hugged me. So did the Upchuck sisters. My mom cried, fearing what it would mean for my ability to get a job.

But I went back to school to take a photography course and actually got a job: the *Portland Press Herald* hired me as a part-time news photographer. They didn't give a shit that I was gay. Neither did anyone else, really.

X and Patti moved in together, in this bricks-and-beams loft place down by Casco Bay. We had great parties there. We danced. We played Scrabble (X always won). X wrote for his magazines, and Patti kept going to school at MSU, studying sociology and women's studies. Patti stuff.

Sister Betty, meanwhile, got accepted to this little university called Harvard to study English. That meant the end of the Punk Rock Virgins, pretty much, but she didn't want to stick around Portland anymore. Just in case Detective Savoie reopened the unsolved Thomas M. Jones murder investigation, she whispered to me, the hot August night we all gathered at Gary's to see her off.

X was there, sipping his RC Cola, unsmiling. Patti was beside him, of course, alternately beaming about her little sister's achievement and tearing up because she was leaving.

Sam Shiller and Luke Macdonald were there, too, with the Hot Nasties' drummer, Jessie. Jessie was out, too, and no one cared about that, either. Certainly not Sam, who was looking at law schools, or Luke, who was working for his dad. The Nasties, we all decided, were going to go back to what the band had been at the start: not a job, not a ticket to the "big time," just punk rock fun.

That night, I looked around Gary's, at the filthy tables, the overflowing ashtrays, the sticky floors. It was still a shithole, this place, but it was our shithole. Our safe punk rock home, like the Clash sang, sort of. I looked around at my friends. We were still punks, we'd always be punks — although, I suspected, marriages and mortgages and even little punk rock babies might be in some of our futures. Not distant futures, either.

Looking at all my friends, I felt emotional. We'd all gone through so much together — the loss of too many friends, the loss of our innocence. As they all chattered amongst themselves, talking about Sister Betty's adventure, about Patti's planned graduate degree, about Sam's plans, and Luke's, X was looking at me. He cocked an eyebrow above those famously uneven pupils.

"It's okay," I said to him, waving a hand. "I was just wondering, as we all get older, if we are ever going to stop being rebels, you know?"

X, my best friend, raised his glass of RC Cola and looked at me. "Never," he said. "To punk rock."

And we toasted punk rock and our friends, those who were there and those we had lost along the way.

"To punk!"

ACKNOWLEDGEMENTS

Thanks to the following for keeping me moving forward: Ras Pierre and Rockin' Al; Bjorn von Flapjack II; Snipe Yeomanson; the Hot Nasties; Shit From Hell; Steve Deceive Ladurantaye; Nick the K; Simon Harvey and Ugly Pop; Ron Ruskin; Snowdy; Brian Goldman; the Farber brothers; Michael Kleinman; Darryl Fine and the Bovine; Amrazment; every new friend in Hillier, my true home; Chief Kelly; Dave Plewes; Babs; the amazing Kane Kinsella; Cherry Cola; Flav; Roxy and Joey; Jay Bentley of Bad Religion; Scott Hutchinson, Alex, and everyone at H and H; Allison Hirst and all the great folks at Dundurn; the Bronx; Laura Jane Grace of Against Me; Terry and Chris and the Patrician gang; Scott Sellers; Jim Lindberg of Pennywise; John Tory and John Jr.; my Green Party pals; Don Guy; Rob Gilmour, Logan Ross, Tom Henheffer, Zach Voth, Zack Babins, Katie Watson, and the entire Daisy gang; my political father, Jean Chrétien; John Walsh; my sister Batra and the video visionary Nelson; Melissa Lantsman; Jamie Wallace; Evan Solomon; Karl Hale; Sylvia; Charles Adler; Doug; my departed brother Gordie; Nick Nelson; Mike Bendixen and Jessie and everyone at 1010; Karl Belanger; my amazing ex, Suze, and her partner, Bruce; John Moore; Lorna, my ever-protective mom; and my awesome regular readers, who are totally awesome.

Most of all, however, I give thanks for my punk rock kids — Emma, Ben, Sam, and Jacob — who give me hope, who give me faith, and who are the ones who never stopped loving me (and who still love Bad Religion, too).

W.K.
TeeDot, 2019